CHARITY
THE SHACKLEFORD SISTERS
BOOK SIX

BEVERLEY WATTS

Copyright © 2023 BaR Publishing

© 2023 BaR Publishing. All rights reserved. No part of this publication may be reproduced, stored or transmitted in any form or by any means, electronic, mechanical, photocopying, recording, scanning or otherwise without written permission from the publisher.

It is illegal to copy this book, post it to a website, or distribute it by any other means without permission.
This novel is entirely a work of fiction. The names, characters and incidents portrayed in it are the work of the author's imagination. Any resemblance to actual persons, living or dead, events or localities is entirely coincidental.

BaR Publishing has no responsibility for the persistence or accuracy of URL's for external or third party Internet Websites referred to in this publication and does not guarantee that any content on such Websites is, or will remain, accurate or appropriate.

Designations used by companies to distinguish their products are often claimed as trademarks. All brand names and product names used in this book and on its cover are trade names, service marks, trademarks and registered trademarks of their respective owners. The publishers and the book are not associated with any product or vendor mentioned in this book. None of the companies referenced within the book have endorsed the book.

Cover art by Midnight Muse
Typography by Covers By Karen

CHAPTER 1

Sitting at his customary table in the Red Lion Inn, Reverend Shackleford took a large sip from his tankard of real ale and congratulated himself on now being in possession of five influential, not to mention, extremely wealthy sons-in-law. His coffers were filling nicely, and soon there'd be enough to ensure that Anthony would be able to take his place in Society - with wealth enough in his own right and not simply as a poor relation. Although being a poor relation to a duke, an earl, a marquess and a viscount was surely not to be sniffed at.

And now, at twelve, the boy was attending daily lessons at Blackmore along with Nicholas and Grace's son Peter. Things were moving along very satisfactorily indeed - apart from the minor fact that according to the boys' tutor, Anthony was not the best of influences on the six-year-old heir to the Duke of Blackmore's estates.

Augustus Shackleford frowned, his good humour souring a little. Truth be told, Anthony was too ripe and ready by half. Hardly surprising given that he'd spent the whole of his childhood trailing after his eight sisters who'd nearly always been up to something and hadn't given a tinker's damn about tying their collective garters in public.

Sighing, the Reverend picked up his tankard. Truly, it had been a long weary road, and he couldn't help feeling he'd spent much of it in one hobble or another. But now, only three of his daughters remained unwed, and he was persuaded that he hadn't made an entire mull of things.

Naturally, it was a little troubling that at eighteen, neither of the twins, Charity and Chastity had shown much inclination towards matrimony. Still, putting aside Charity's tendency to be disturbingly forthright, he was assured that both girls were more than passably pretty, and he had high hopes that one of them at least might brave the marriage mart.

Reverend Shackleford took another contented sip of his ale having no doubt that one of his sons-in-law would eventually put his hand in his purse to furnish the chits with a London Season.

Inevitably, his thoughts then turned to Prudence, and he gave a small shudder before rallying. At sixteen there was still time to take her in hand. Hurriedly dismissing the unsettling thoughts of his youngest daughter lest they give him an ulcer, Augustus Shackleford returned his deliberations to his only son.

Anthony was simply displaying the same tendencies as any young man. Pushing boundaries was what young gentlemen did, he was certain. Though in fairness, he wasn't actually acquainted with any young gentlemen of his son's age to confirm such a theory. Frowning, he thought again of his daughters. They hadn't so much pushed boundaries as simply ridden over them. Still, young men were expected to be boisterous, and he would have a chat with Anthony, man to man, this very evening.

Indeed, it felt as if the Almighty was finally about to reward him for his unwavering dedication. Waving his hand towards the innkeeper,

Reverend Shackleford decided to treat himself to a steak and kidney pudding in celebration, entirely certain the worst was over.

∞∞∞

The weather was unseasonably warm for February, so much so that wild crocuses and daffodils were even now blooming in the hedgerows and fields around Blackmore. It was a far cry from the bloody war that had been raging in Europe for over twenty years. But for the first time, it seemed there was a light at the end of the tunnel. Back in October, Napoleon had finally been defeated at the Battle of Leipzig, ensuring the collapse of the French Empire east of the Rhine. The self-styled emperor was being slowly forced back towards Paris with the coalition armies comprising Russia, Prussia, Austria and Sweden in hot pursuit. Reports coming through declared that the Duke of Wellington was already in southwestern France with his forces, having pushed French troops out of Spain and was on his way to Paris. The news sheets were declaring the war all but over.

Grace watched as her husband's carriage finally disappeared through the distant gates that formed the entrance and exit to the Blackmore estate. Although she and Nicholas had been married for nigh on eight years, she never grew accustomed to his enforced absences and, in truth, she knew it was the same for him.

On this occasion, the situation in Europe was dragging him away from Blackmore and finally the news was good. Napoleon was on the run, and it seemed as though it was only a matter of time before he would be forced to abdicate. Nicholas had been called to an urgent meeting of the Lords to be held at Westminster.

It was not so bad. While Nicholas would be away for some weeks, she would be joining him in just over a month. Indeed, practically her whole family would be congregating for the first time since Patience's wedding to the Marquess of Guildford eighteen months earlier.

In the wake of that marriage, the cold shoulder previously offered to the entire Shackleford family by Queen Charlotte had finally been put to bed. Even more surprising was the unexpected shine her majesty had taken to Patience. Seating herself by the fire, Grace chuckled to herself. Though her sister had almost certainly not meant to be funny, Patience had on one particular occasion announced to her Majesty that the Lord Steward reminded her of their foxhound, Freddy.

So here they all were, back in Charlotte's good books. Until the next time…

The only ones missing from the reunion in London would be Faith and Roan as her sister had recently delivered of a healthy baby girl. It was for that reason that Grace had been persuaded that two of the four weeks away from her husband would be most agreeably spent visiting Torquay and her new niece.

The Duchess glanced over at her own daughter, busy cleaning the morning room windows with a napkin. Wincing at the revolting looking smudges smeared across the glass, Grace reflected it was unfortunate that the napkin had earlier been used to remove the remains of Mrs Higgins' prize-winning chocolate cake from the little girl's fingers.

Almost three now, Jennifer was already exhibiting slightly alarming traits comparable to those displayed by the rest of the females in her family. Grace shook her head with a rueful smile. Really, Nicholas was entirely too soft on her.

A sudden knock on the door brought her out of her reverie. 'Come,' she announced, pouring herself another dish of tea.

The door opened to reveal Jimmy, her husband's … well his general *do all* she supposed. Nobody seemed at all certain exactly what it was that Jimmy actually did for Nicholas. When asked, the Duke generally laughed and winked. Grace knew her husband was very fond of the rascal and suspected he kept the boy close to ensure the rogue stayed on a path of … well, if not righteousness, then straight enough to keep his head out of the noose. The Duke's patronage also ensured that Jimmy's widowed mother had enough food on her table.

She looked over at the boy, politely doffing his cap. In truth, Jimmy was no longer a lad. He was filling out, and at nearly eighteen with hair the colour of old gold and cornflower blue eyes, he was already catching the eye of every unmarried female within a five-mile radius.

'Beggin yer pardon, yer grace,' he murmured, 'Miss Charity charged me wi' delivering 'er note.' He held out an envelope. 'She said it were to go into no one's hand but yer grace's.'

Grace frowned and held out her hand, wondering if her sister had a problem. Things had actually been unusually peaceful at the vicarage since Patience's marriage. If the twins had been up to some mischief, they had kept remarkably quiet about it. But then at eighteen, they were grown women and like to put such childish pursuits aside. As she slit open the letter, Grace determinedly ignored the small voice in her head that pointed out that becoming an adult had in no way curbed her own tendency for mischief.

'Damn and blast,' she muttered on reading the contents.

The twins might be considered women grown, but neither Charity nor Chastity had expressed any wish for a Season in London – or anywhere else for that matter - and aside from the fact that she wished her sisters to make good marriages, Grace had learned from the mistakes she had made when forcing Patience down a path she had no wish to tread. The fact that it had worked out so well, was most definitely not due to either her or Tempy's machinations. Nevertheless, she had high hopes that in another year or two, the twins might reconsider.

However, on reading the note in her hand, she couldn't help but wonder if her restraint had on this occasion backfired spectacularly.

∞∞∞∞

'True love knows no boundaries,' Chastity declared dramatically, her hand fluttering around the area she supposed her heart to be.

'Oh don't be such a complete mutton head,' snorted Charity. 'The only words you've exchanged are about the deuced weather.' She paused and gritted her teeth in frustration. She loved her twin sister dearly, but Chastity's proclivity for seeing romance in any male under the age of sixty in possession of his own teeth was tiresome to say the least. She sat down on the vicarage parlour's chaise longue, usually occupied by their stepmother Agnes. On this occasion the matron had decided to take her afternoon nap in her bedchamber. Which was fortunate given the current subject matter over tea.

'And besides,' Charity continued, her voice turning desperate, 'the person you are speaking of resides in a one-bedroom cottage which he shares with his mother and three sisters.'

Chastity frowned. 'He does?'

Charity nodded, wondering if she was finally getting through. Really, she wished her sister had agreed to a season in London. As romantic as she was, Chastity would almost certainly snare herself, if not a Lord, then at least someone of fairly reasonable means.

Unfortunately, Charity's own refusal to take part in the marriage mart had her younger twin nobly sacrificing herself to spinsterhood. The words *noble* and *sacrifice* had been accompanied by the dramatic declaration that she would simply *die* before abandoning the person she described as, amongst other things ... *closest to her heart; her other half; the sun to her moon; the night to her* ... Charity wasn't sure what. At this point she'd given up listening.

Charity sighed. Of the two of them, Chastity was far more suited to matrimony. Unfortunately, it was beginning to look as if the only way the silly goose was ever likely to find a man even remotely suitable, was if she herself agreed to partake of a London Season alongside her twin. She frowned, suddenly realising Chastity was speaking again.

'Well, Mr Timson informed me that he had been offered a dependency in Brixham. He was most insistent that it would be accompanied by a small apartment.'

Charity frowned. If her sister had indulged in an actual conversation with the odious toad that was Obadiah Timson, then things were much worse than she thought.

'When did you have this conversation with Mr Timson?' she queried, taking care to keep her tone light and conversational, while inside, her stomach was roiling sickeningly. Her twin coloured up, and Charity's heart plummeted to join the party. 'We simply took a walk after church on Sunday,' Chastity explained.

'You said you were going to take a slice of apple pie to Mrs Peterson in the village,' Charity accused.

'Well, I did,' Chastity retorted. 'Mr Timson was kind enough to walk me there.'

Charity stared at her sister in horror. 'For goodness' sake, Chastity, what the deuce were you thinking?' she bit out, fighting to hold her temper. 'Father will be furious when he finds out. You'll be lucky if he doesn't confine you to the attic for the next six months. Have you lost what little wit you have?'

'I should think he'd be more likely to pack you off to Mrs Brandreth's Seminary for Fallen Women,' commented a new voice from the doorway.' Both twins turned to their sister Prudence as she continued into the parlour and helped herself to a biscuit from the tray.

'Aren't you supposed to be going to fetch Anthony from Blackmore?' questioned Charity tartly.

'I saw a pamphlet in his study,' Prudence continued nonchalantly, ignoring her sister's query.

'What pamphlet? I've never heard of such a place.' Charity's voice was scathing but underneath was a thread of doubt.

'You'll be forced to scrub floors from dawn until dusk, then fed bread and water before being dragged abed. A bit like that horrible place Patience was imprisoned.'

'Don't be so ridiculous, Pru,' Charity retorted. 'There is no such place.'

Prudence shrugged and took another biscuit. 'Have a look for yourself,' she suggested. 'The pamphlet's sitting on his desk.'

'What were you doing in Father's study anyway?' demanded Chastity, trying to force away lurid visions involving a scrubbing brush.

'I was looking for Freddy,' Prudence responded. 'I thought to take him with me to collect Anthony.'

'I'm certain you are fully aware that Father's in the Red Lion,' answered Charity. 'And will undoubtedly have Freddy with him.' She gave her sister a challenging stare.

'Well, that will give you plenty of time to remove the pamphlet from Father's desk then, won't it?' Prudence declared with a wicked grin, before heading back out of the door.

'We really shouldn't have taken it,' whispered Chastity an hour later. They were seated in their bedchamber with the offending circular on the bed between them.

'I've no idea why you're whispering,' grumbled Charity. 'It's not as if anyone is likely to hear you. And anyway, do you really want to risk having…' she paused and peered down at the piece of paper on the bed… 'the evils of your mind put aside in favour of hard labour and prayer?' Chastity shook her head mutely as her sister sat back on her heels.

'Well, if Father finds out about Obadiah Timson, you might as well start preparing your knees for calluses right now.' Charity knew she was being harsh. She also knew that the prospect of their father deciding to send one of his daughters to an institute for fallen women was about as likely as him marrying one of them off to Percy. She frowned. That said, the pamphlet *was* on his desk…

'What are we going to do?' Chastity breathed, fighting back tears.

Charity sighed and shook her head. 'What we always do,' she muttered. 'Send a note to Grace…'

CHAPTER 2

'Oh, Chastity,' Grace remonstrated. 'What on earth were you thinking?'

'He told me I was pretty,' faltered Chastity.

'Is your head so easily turned, you would heed the words of any sweet-tongued numbskull?' Charity flung back, unable to stifle her irritation at her sister's foolishness.

The twins had been received in the morning room at Blackmore having sent the missive to their eldest sister the afternoon before. Grace had wasted no time in responding and the seal on her reply to their note made it clear that she was speaking as the Duchess. Her invitation to attend her at Blackmore the following morning was a command, not a request.

'Bickering will get us nowhere,' Grace sighed, picking up her dish of tea. 'I think you'd better start at the beginning Chastity.' She paused and narrowed her eyes, before warning, 'It will serve no purpose to leave anything out. I cannot deal with what I do not know.'

Fifteen minutes later, Grace was white faced and Charity was glaring at her sister in unaccustomed anger.

'You allowed him to *kiss* you? Are you completely bacon-brained? *Obadiah Timson*. Please tell me you're aware the oily snake counts half the girls in the village his conquests?'

'He *is* very handsome,' Chastity defended. She creased her brow. 'But in truth, the kiss was a little … disappointing. His lips were dry … and … well, a bit … crusted.'

Both listeners recoiled at the conjured picture. Indeed, Grace had to swallow hard as her earlier toast threatened to make a sudden reappearance.

'I know I've been foolish,' Chastity whispered as she registered the appalled expressions of her sisters. 'You can rest assured I will tell Mr Timson I have no wish to see or speak with him again.'

'You will do no such thing,' snapped Grace, collecting herself. 'You will neither see, nor speak with Mr Timson *ever* again.' She raised her eyes to the heavens while thanking her lucky stars that on this occasion Nicholas wasn't here. That said, deciding what to do with her idiot sister without his matter-of-fact counsel…

She gave a loud sigh. Obadiah Timson's face might well be agreeable, but according to Jimmy, his personality was anything but, and Grace had no doubt such an obnoxious individual would endeavour to create trouble, especially in the Master of Blackmore's absence. Naturally, they had to remove Chastity from the vicinity at the earliest opportunity. That in itself wasn't a problem. Chastity could accompany her to Faith and Roan's. An extra pair of hands would be most welcome.

The more pressing concern was whether to involve their father or not…

∞∞∞

'Are you there Percy?' The Reverend peered into the gloom of the church vestry. None of the candles were lit which was unusual in itself at three in the afternoon. Normally, Percy could be entirely relied upon to be exactly where he should be at any given time of the day. Reverend Shackleford frowned. However, it was blatantly obvious that his curate was not, on this occasion, exactly where he should be. Deuced inconsiderate man. Glancing down at Freddy, he had a sudden idea. If Percy was off gallivanting, then the foxhound's legendary nose would almost certainly discover where in no time at all. Especially as Percy was one of his favourite humans.

Stepping into the vestry, Augustus Shackleford looked around for something small belonging to his curate. As his eyes became accustomed to the mid-afternoon shadows, he noticed a paper on the desk. Thinking it a first draft of Sunday's sermon, the Reverend hurried over. Mayhap a quick read now would forestall too many lurid descriptions of the afterlife facing Blackmore's residents if they continued on their wicked path. Trying to dilute Percy's messages of doom and gloom was challenging as a rule, and even more so when the Reverend's first read through was in the pulpit…

Hurrying over to the desk, the Reverend picked up the single sheet of paper. If it was the first draft of Sunday's sermon, then Percy hadn't got very far. His curate's usual wont was at twelve pages at least, ofttimes more. Muttering, the Reverend searched in his pockets for his eyeglasses. The dratted things were never where they were supposed to be. Finally locating them, he placed them on his nose and stared down at the paper in his hand. It was a letter.

Without any qualms, he read Percy's scrawling handwriting. Slowly, a cold sweat broke out on his forehead. Just when he believed his problems were over. He glanced upwards and sighed. Truly, he should have known better. If he'd learned anything during his time as a man of the cloth, it was that the Almighty had an unlikely sense of humour.

∞∞∞

'What do you mean Percy's gone?' Grace's incredulity could not have been greater had her father informed her that the curate had suddenly found himself a wife. 'Where has he gone?'

Reverend Shackleford squirmed uncomfortably. 'I believe he decided to visit his mother in Salcombe.'

'He has a mother?' Charity's interjection showed exactly the same astonishment.

'Well he wasn't delivered by a stork,' the Reverend muttered, exasperation overtaking his discomfort.

'I believed him an orphan.' Grace frowned. 'I certainly had no idea he had family living so close. Why does he not pay her regular visits?'

'Erm ... I believe they err ..., that is ... I'm given to understand that Percy's mother is not of the same persuasion.'

'She's a Roman Catholic?'

'Not exactly.'

'Well, she either is or she isn't,' Grace snapped. 'Which is it?'

Reverend Shackleford felt himself begin to sweat under his cassock. If there had been any way to keep his daughter in the dark, he would have done so. Unfortunately, their only horse, a bad-tempered stallion aptly named Lucifer, had been put out to pasture six months earlier so his only method of getting to Salcombe was by carriage. Specifically one belonging to the Duke of Blackmore.

'Percy's mother is not of a religious persuasion.' The Reverend ensured his voice showed the sorrow appropriate to his distress at the likely direction Mrs Noon's immortal soul would travel after she kicked the bucket.

'Is she on her deathbed then?' Charity questioned. 'Has Percy gone to pray for her?'

The Reverend nodded fervently. 'Unquestionably.' The relief in his voice had both daughters regarding him doubtfully. 'What kind of a friend would I be were I not prepared to drop everything to provide what comfort I can in his time of need?'

'You have a duty to your parishioners,' protested Grace. 'What of them?'

'I will not be gone long,' the Reverend declared. 'I will ensure my duties are taken care of in my absence. In fact, I believe his mother will be departing this mortal coil and in the arms of the Almighty any day now.'

'I thought you said she wasn't religious,' Charity retorted.

'She isn't *yet*,' her father responded through gritted teeth.

'I would have thought Percy is more than capable of seeing to his mother's last rites,' retorted Grace. 'He certainly has more piety than you do Father.'

Reverend Shackleford gave an indignant hmph, offering up an internal prayer for the slight untruths he was being *forced* to utter while at the same time asking to be delivered from deuced interfering daughters.

'I am certain it will be no more than a matter of days. Agnes will not be alone. After all, you and your sister are ladies now, Charity, and able to provide … err … womanly diversions to keep your stepmother entertained.'

Charity snorted. 'The only items Stepmother needs to keep her entertained are her periodicals and her smelling salts, and Prudence is more than capable of providing both.' She shook her head. 'I think I should come with you, Father.'

'Absolutely not.' The Reverend's vehement response increased his two daughters' suspicions.

'What are you not telling us, Father?' Grace queried, her eyes narrowing.

'What about Chastity?' The Reverend countered instead of answering the question. 'You wouldn't wish to leave your twin. You're usually joined at the deuced hip. And of a certainty, I cannot take you both.' He paused, then narrowed his eyes in return, suddenly aware of an inconsistency. 'And anyway, why must Prudence be the one to provide succour to your stepmother?'

'Chastity is coming with me to Faith's,' Grace declared abruptly.

Augustus Shackleford frowned, sensing something amiss. 'Why only Chastity?' he queried. 'Would not both girls benefit from some sea air?'

'It would be entirely too much for Faith in her delicate situation,' Grace responded briskly. 'I think Charity will be better placed with you.' She got to her feet, signifying an end to the conversation. 'I will have Mrs Tenner put together some medicinal supplies to help with any pain.' She glanced over at her sister. 'Charity is eminently capable of providing the necessary assistance.'

Then without giving her father time to respond, she swept out of the room, Charity at her heels, leaving the Reverend pondering which of them had just been fed the larger bag of moonshine.

∞∞∞

Seated comfortably in the Duke of Blackmore's second-best carriage the following morning, Charity closed her eyes and feigned sleep. The last thing she wanted was an interrogation, and even behind her closed lids, she could sense her father eying her speculatively. He was a master at diverting attention from his own Banbury stories by focusing on someone else's.

Cuddling Freddy to her, and revelling in the warmth the foxhound supplied, Charity's thoughts turned to her twin sister. Father was right. They'd been practically inseparable throughout the whole of their lives. Unlike Faith and Hope, their older twin siblings, Charity and Chastity were almost identical. In thought as well as looks.

Until Patience's unexpected wedding. In the last eighteen months *something* had changed. Oh they still finished one another's sentences, laughed at the same things, enjoyed ribbing Anthony, ran rings around their father and stepmother. But something was different. It was as though, of a sudden, their paths had begun to separate.

They'd both always enjoyed reading, very often the same book at the same time, but after Patience left, Chastity's taste began to lean more towards romance - much of it entirely unsuitable reading matter for a clergyman's daughter. She always seemed to be swooning over some imaginary hero - handsome naturally.

Up until Patience's wedding, both girls had spent much of their time outdoors and were rarely inside the vicarage in between breakfast and supper. But lately, Chastity had been looking for excuses to remain inside. She would avidly pour over their stepmother's periodicals and gossip sheets, endlessly talking about Lord this and Viscount that. Her sudden onset of dreaminess set Charity's teeth on edge. And now the family was back in Queen Charlotte's good books, their older sisters had naturally mooted the opportunity of a Season in London.

Once upon a time, both twins would have been horrified at the very idea. But now, Charity knew very well that the only reason Chastity had poo pooed the prospect was out of loyalty to her twin, dramatic though her denouement had been.

It wasn't that Charity was against the idea of marriage. She certainly didn't have the same aversion Patience had displayed and was pragmatic enough to know they couldn't stay under their father's roof forever. But since every one of their older siblings had achieved advantageous unions, indeed, wildly beyond anyone's expectations, Charity had felt as if a noose was tightening around her neck. What if she went through the rigmarole of a season and nobody offered for her? She wasn't stupid and was well aware that she and her twin were possessed of more than passable looks. Both boasted a pleasingly thick head of chestnut hair that took a curl nicely. Clear skin and nicely rounded curves. That was what Tempy said anyway.

But while Chastity was possessed of a sunny disposition to go with her romantic notions and pretty face, Charity's wit most definitely veered towards sarcasm, but worse than that was her complete inability to stifle her honesty. Plain speaking had got her into trouble on so many occasions, though Chastity had loyally taken the blame for at least some of her twin's faux pas. In that way, Charity supposed she was a little similar to Patience. Though unlike her older sister, she enjoyed the company of others and was not *intentionally* rude.

Sighing internally, Charity's thoughts came back to the present. She realised she was being entirely unfair towards her twin through her unwillingness to play the marriage mart. And Chastity's idealistic, not to mention her absurdly trusting nature had already got her into trouble. Of course it could have been considerably worse, and next time… Charity shuddered inwardly. This could not be allowed to go on. As soon as she and her father returned from Salcombe, she would send a note to Grace concerning the possibility of a Season. Hopefully, before Chastity ended up ruining herself.

CHAPTER 3

*J*ago Carlyon, stepped into the dim interior of the Seven Stars Inn in the fishing port of Dartmouth and waited for his eyes to adjust to the meagre light. He'd been given instructions to meet at five o'clock, but Jago had chosen to arrive well ahead of the assignation. Perhaps he was being over careful, but such caution had saved his life on more than one occasion. Taking his tankard of ale to the very back of the pub, he took a seat in a discreet corner, his chair facing out into the room. The inn was quiet with only a few fishermen congregating around the bar. Jago knew he would attract more than a few surreptitious glances, but he was known well enough in the area to alleviate the misgivings of all but the most suspicious locals.

Naturally, if the inhabitants of the tavern had been aware of Jago's true reason for being there, they might well have given him a much wider berth. As it was, they supposed him a simple labourer, albeit a well-mannered one and assumed he was treating himself to a well-earned tankard of ale after a hard day.

As it was, they were wrong on both counts. Indeed, they believed his name to be Cardell, but that was as fictitious as his occupation. Oh, he helped offload the cargo of the merchant ships docked by the quayside well enough, but that was to cover up his true purpose for being in Dartmouth.

But now, after two years living in the shadows, Jago believed he was finally close to unmasking the man who'd murdered his sister.

∞∞∞

Against the odds, Charity actually did fall asleep, lulled by the rhythmic rocking of the carriage. As she woke, she thought for a second that she and Chastity were on their way to Ravenstone. When memory came crashing back, she was consumed by a sudden sense of loss. Exasperating though Chastity very often was, Charity suddenly found herself missing her twin fiercely.

Reluctantly opening her eyes, Charity leaned forward to look out of the window. The scenery was much as before, rolling green hills and tall hedgerows giving no clue as to how far along their journey they were. However, the watery sun was now much lower in the sky indicating they were well into the afternoon.

Picking at the bread and cheese Mrs Tomlinson had packed for them, Charity regarded her father as he sat snoring opposite. This was almost certainly the first occasion she'd spent time alone in his company. Indeed, over the years, she and her twin had almost perfected the art of avoiding their irascible parent outside of supper. Sighing, she broke off a piece of cheese and handed it to Freddy, who was lying sprawled across her lap, a veritable fur blanket.

Stroking his head gently, she wondered about Percy's mother. Hopefully, the elderly matron would not have departed to her reward before she and her father got there. Charity had never been to Salcombe. She was aware that the small fishing village was situated on the south Devon coast, close to the larger ports of Kingsbridge and Dartmouth, but she'd had no idea that Percy had relatives there. It was difficult to actually imagine her father's curate as a child, he'd simply been a part of her life since she could remember. He was … well, he was … *Percy*.

A long sigh brought her head up from the rough fur of the foxhound. Her father was awake and staring out of the carriage window, his brow creased as though the weight of the world was on his shoulders. Unexpectedly, she felt a stirring of sympathy. Her father must be worried indeed to have dropped everything to rush to Percy's aid. It certainly showed that, while he might not exhibit much compassion outwardly, he obviously cared deeply about his curate.

'I'm sure Percy will be extremely grateful for your presence, Father, at such a difficult time,' Charity murmured softly.

At first, she thought he hadn't heard, but after a few seconds, he turned towards her and shook his head before speaking. 'There's no sense beating around the deuced bush,' he declared, the brusqueness in his voice causing Charity's heart to stutter unpleasantly. 'You might as well know what we're getting ourselves into.'

'I'm no stranger to a sick bed, Father,' she interrupted bravely.

His answer was a rude snort. 'Then it's good you won't be attending one. Old Mrs Noon's not about to cash in her chips, though that might well change pretty sharpish if I don't put a good word in for her.'

Charity frowned. 'Couldn't you have done that at home, Father? I mean after all, surely the best place for prayer is in the church.'

'Mary Noon's soul is not a discussion the Almighty and I are likely to have anytime soon,' retorted the Reverend. 'And anyway, that's Percy's job. If there's an outside chance of his mother slipping through the back door to the heavenly hereafter, I'm certain Percy will find it.'

Charity stared at him nonplussed. 'Then why are you rushing to her aid?' she queried, 'If not God, who are you intending to petition?'

'The Custom's officer in Dartmouth,' her father responded flatly. 'Mary was caught with half a dozen bladders of brandy sewn inside her stays. It's a wonder she managed to walk at all.'

∞∞∞

In the end, the extra precautions Jago took were for naught. The man did not turn up. Though inwardly seething, he made sure to stay until nearly closing time. It would not have done to arrive and leave before the busy period. People tended to remember. He ordered ham and eggs for his supper, taking care to give just enough attention to the young and attractive bar maid. It wasn't difficult. She still had most of her teeth and her smile hadn't yet become too jaded.

Finally heading out into the chill, damp air, Jago briefly allowed his frustration to swamp him. And that small loss of concentration was all it took. In seconds, an arm snaked around his neck and a knife was at his throat.

'You waitin' fer someone?' whispered a voice in his ear. Rancid breath drifted towards his nose, almost making him gag. Cursing inwardly, Jago forced down his fury and self-contempt at being caught with his proverbial britches down. All his caution wasted in a momentary fit of petulance. The street was deserted, so help of any kind was unlikely.

Jago took as deep a breath as he dared with the edge of the knife digging into the tender skin at his throat. Fighting for calm, he spoke, keeping his voice low and composed. 'I had a meeting with Jack.'

'Says who?' The arm tightened, and Jago felt his anger rise. 'You know who I am,' he whispered through gritted teeth. 'If you didn't, you'd have slit my throat by now. Take me to Jack, and be done with it. I have information for him.' He paused and felt the sweat begin beading on his forehead as the knife pressed harder into his neck.

'Tell him I want in. He won't regret it,' Jago ground out, trying not to let desperation colour his voice. There was a silence behind him, then slowly, the shadowy figure stepped back and lowered the knife. Jago took a deep breath and clenched his hands to stop their trembling. Stepping carefully out of reach, he slowly pivoted until he was facing his attacker.

'Jack ain't comin'. He sent me instead.'

Jago ground his teeth in frustration. It had taken nearly two years to get this far. But now, finally, when he was about to discover the elusive Jack's real identity, the bastard had slipped out of his reach again. He eyed the sorry-looking individual watching him. It was almost pitch black, the only light coming from the Seven Stars behind the man, but it was enough to reveal a tall skinny individual in tattered clothing with a face that had likely last seen water years ago. It was clear the man was completely expendable to the mysterious leader of the smuggling ring working this stretch of coast.

'Tell Jack I want in,' he repeated as evenly as his thudding heart would allow. 'I have information he'll want, but I'm not giving it to a bloody lackey. It's face-to-face or nothing.'

'You ain't got no chance o' that,' the messenger sneered. 'Jack don't jump for the likes o'you.'

Jago shook his head, then took a chance. 'Trust works both ways,' he bit out. 'I have something Jack wants. He has something I want. Tell him, all he has to do is let me in, and I swear I'll make us both rich.'

∞∞∞

After barely scratching the surface of *what they were getting into*, her father had been disinclined to answer any more questions aside from informing her they were heading for Dartmouth rather than Salcombe since that was where Mary Noon was incarcerated. At length, Charity subsided into frustrated silence. She wondered what on earth Grace would have to say when she found out.

As if he could read her mind, her father elicited her promise that under no circumstances was she to mention their true mission to another living soul. *Especially* not her eldest sister. And *most expressly* not her eldest sister's husband.

In a flurry of sudden enlightenment, Charity eyed her father narrowly. 'Why exactly do you wish me to keep silent, Father?' she demanded. 'Could it be because you are a recipient of Mrs Noon's ill-gotten gains perchance?'

The Reverend's indignant splutter gave him away. 'Does Percy know you use his mother as a … a … contraband supplier?' she probed, aghast.

Her father hmphed, his discomfort a palpable thing. But he said nothing.

'I'll wager he doesn't,' she continued, getting into her stride. 'You are a man of the cloth, Father. I cannot conceive how you can possibly think it right and proper to purchase smuggled goods. If you're not careful, you could end up in the cell next door to Percy's mother.'

'I only take the occasional bottle,' Reverend Shackleford defended finally, his voice that of a sulky twelve-year-old, 'just to help Percy's old mother a little. She doesn't have much, and…'

'Don't you dare make this sound as though you are doing this out of the goodness of your heart, Father. No wonder you've come running. It has nothing to do with your concern for Percy and everything to do with your fear of being rumbled.'

They both subsided into an uneasy silence until, at length, the Reverend sighed and spoke. 'You're right in everything you said,' he admitted. 'But in truth, I was *mainly* doing it to help Percy's mother. She hasn't got two ha' pennies to rub together.' He shrugged. 'The brandy's all very well, but you forget I have five sons-in-law who would be more than happy to keep me in my cups until the day I'm ready for a tipple with the Almighty.'

He shook his head before continuing ruefully, 'We don't talk about it. But I think Percy knows. That's why he left without speaking to me first.'

Charity shook her head, only slightly mollified. Apprehension warred with frustration. She'd thought them on a mercy mission, but now… She had no idea what was waiting for them in Dartmouth, and she was ill equipped to deal with anything other than mopping brows or changing dressings. She and her sister might have been involved in all manner of scrapes over the years, but they'd never actually done anything illegal.

She gave a vexed sigh. There was no sense in continuing the argument with her father. It wouldn't change the position they were in. Grimacing, she handed the rest of the bread and cheese to Freddy, having completely lost her appetite.

For the next hour they sat in silence, but as late afternoon slipped into twilight, Charity suggested they stop the carriage before it became too dark to allow Freddy to do his business. Unfortunately, as soon as the dog was allowed out of the carriage, he disappeared into the hedgerow, and they spent a tense thirty minutes waiting for the disobedient foxhound to return. Going after the hound had been out of the question lest one or both of them become hopelessly lost.

Full dark had descended by the time Freddy finally reappeared by the side of the carriage, but both the Reverend and Charity were too relieved by his sudden reappearance to scold the dog unduly.

Until the smells started.

'I think he might have eaten something too long dead,' muttered the Reverend, wrinkling his nose the first time. Charity didn't risk speaking as to do so would have involved inhaling through her nose. Instead, she held a kerchief to her face in an effort to reduce the awful stench, though she could do nothing to stem her watering eyes.

By the time the carriage finally negotiated the steep rutted track that was the only access down into Dartmouth, the stink had become so noxious that Charity was convinced she was about to cast up her account. The only positive in the whole sorry business was that Freddy had so far refused to deposit the results of his bad stomach within the confines of the carriage.

'We have to stop, Father,' Charity mumbled through her kerchief. 'Poor Freddy must be in terrible pain.'

'I'll give the sorry hound "poor Freddy,"' the Reverend retorted, rapping on the roof to get the coachman's attention. Obligingly, the driver pulled onto the side of the road conveniently close to a large open space. Fumbling with the door, Charity finally managed to get it open and stumbled out but not before the foxhound had disappeared into the darkness.

'I'm too old for gallivanting around the deuced countryside,' the Reverend muttered as he climbed laboriously down after her. Charity didn't answer, being too busy drawing as much mercifully fresh air into her starving lungs as she could.'

'Might I be of any assistance?'

The disembodied voice was loud, cultured and unmistakeably masculine.

CHAPTER 4

The only response from his attacker was a disbelieving snort, and with a last mocking glare, he turned and melded with the darkness, leaving Jago inwardly cursing. Stuffing his hands deep into his pockets, he forced down the rage at being thwarted yet again. Now, more than ever it was essential he keep a level head. Lying in an alley with his damned throat cut was not how he'd envisioned his mission ending.

Sighing, Jago began the long walk back to his accommodation, weary to the bone. God's teeth how he missed Tredennick. But no matter how strong his longing, he could not return to his home in Cornwall until he'd brought justice for his sister.

In truth, it didn't feel like two years since Genevieve had died. For the thousandth time, Jago thought back to the day they'd learned her death had not been an accident. She'd been pushed off that cliff. Her only crime being aboard a vessel thought to hold a cargo of tea.

Genevieve had been staying with friends in London when the merchant ship *Endeavour* put into port. After unloading her cargo, the ship was bound for her captain's home port of Falmouth. As an old family friend, Captain Johnson had offered to bring Genevieve home to Tredennick, a mere stone's throw from Falmouth. Doing the journey by ship would be more comfortable and much quicker than overland by carriage.

Clearly the information received by the smugglers had been false. There was no tea aboard the *Endeavour*, but it did not stop their leader ordering the death of everyone aboard. Afterwards, the ship was scuttled, and the story spread that the vessel had gone down with all hands in a storm.

Tragic though the news was, it would have ended there had not someone aboard the ship survived to bring home the truth. Genevieve Carlyon had been murdered, along with her maid, the Captain and all but one of the crew.

When that knowledge reached Jago's father, the distress tragically brought on an apoplexy, rendering his legs completely useless. To his shame, Morgan Carlyon was forced to remain in his bed while his son pursued the vengeance he could not.

Sighing, Jago forced his thoughts back to the present. He could not help his father walk again, but he hoped that sending Genevieve's killer to the gallows would bring him at least a measure of peace.

As Jago approached his lodgings, he saw a carriage heading towards him, its outline provided by the wavering lamps attached to the driver's box. Frowning, he paused, wondering where the carriage was headed. Even in the meagre light, he could tell it was no hackney coach. And the hour was late.

All of a sudden, the carriage stopped, the door opened and out sprang a dog, quickly disappearing into the undergrowth at the side of the road. The animal was followed immediately afterwards by a young woman. After staggering down from the carriage, she leaned against it and began taking deep shuddering breaths, clearly in distress. Concerned, Jago made his way towards the stationary vehicle, just as an older man began climbing down the steps.

'Might I be of assistance?' he enquired in a loud voice. Startled, the woman turned towards him, and in the paltry light of the carriage lamp, he could see that she was young but very little else. 'Don't come any closer,' she shouted in a frantic voice.

'You have no cause for concern, my lady,' Jago responded, stopping as she requested. 'I was merely returning to my lodgings and saw you descend from your carriage. Your demeanour indicated some discomfort, and I was …' He stopped as the ghastliest smell suddenly reached his nose. Instinctively, he held the back of his hand up against his face. What the devil? Did they have a dead body inside the carriage?

'The deuced dog ate some carrion we think,' clarified the man who he could now see was a man of the cloth. 'I'm not sure we'll ever get the stink out. Nicholas is not going to be happy.'

Jago turned his head to where he'd seen the dog vanish. There was no sign of the hound.

'We'll have to look for him, Father,' the female declared. 'I just hope he manages to purge whatever he's eaten out of his system.'

'It's my experience that animals are a lot more proficient in ridding themselves of poison than humans,' offered Jago solicitously. The woman turned towards him, her face registering surprise that he was still here.

Unaccountably irked that she had so quickly forgotten his presence, he added, 'Would you like my assistance to look for him?'

They both spoke at the same time.

'That will not be…'

'That would be very…'

Halting, the father and daughter stared at each other. 'Well I'm too old to be crawling around in deuced bushes,' the man muttered.

'We don't know who he is,' insisted the woman in a loud whisper he could hear perfectly well. 'He could be intending to murder us ... or worse...'

Shaking his head, Jago fought the urge to simply walk away. He was tired, and narrowly escaping death had left him not a little tetchy.

'Madam,' he snapped, 'if I'd had nefarious designs on your person, I would not be wasting time in polite conversation.'

'D'ye reckon we can get a bloody move on, I'm freezing me ballocks off up 'ere.'

Jago looked up incredulously at the coachman, unsure he'd actually heard him correctly. But before he had the chance to reprimand the man's use of such foul language in front of gentle ears, the woman looked up and *apologised*. 'Forgive me, John, I forgot you've done the whole of the journey outside. I will endeavour to find Freddy as quickly as possible.'

'At least he didn't have to risk death by pestilential vapours,' muttered the clergyman behind her.

Ignoring her father, the lady turned towards Jago. 'If you still find yourself able to assist in looking for Freddy, your help will be most welcome.' She gave an uncertain pause. 'My name is Charity Shackleford, and this is my father, the Reverend Augustus Shackleford. We are most grateful to you, sir.'

Jago raised his eyebrows. *Shackleford*. He'd heard that name somewhere before. He shrugged and dismissed the notion. 'Jago... Cardell at your service my lady.' He gave a slight bow hoping they hadn't noticed his infinitesimal pause before giving his family name. He could not risk being unmasked after so long. He looked up at the coachman. 'If you would allow me the use of one of the lamps, I believe we will have much more success in finding the hound.'

The coachman sighed, and unhooked the lamp nearest to them, then leaning down, placed it in Jago's reaching hand.

'Father, I suggest you get out of the cold and retire to the carriage. Hopefully, the smell will be a little sweeter by now.'

The Reverend hesitated, clearly uncertain as to whether he was placing his daughter in the hands of a knave.

'For goodness' sake, Father,' she snapped, observing his indecision, 'now is not the time to suddenly turn strait-laced. We are in a hobble. And the longer we stand around arguing, the longer it's going to take us to find Freddy.'

The Reverend huffed, muttering, 'You've changed your tune girl. Well don't you be taken in by his deuced pretty face.' Nevertheless, he turned and began climbing back into the carriage.

'Shall we, madam?' Jago murmured, ignoring the pinkness of her cheeks highlighted in the lamplight. Her father's words no doubt. She said nothing, simply pursed her lips, picked up her skirts and marched towards the shadowy copse into which the hound had disappeared.

'Freddy,' she called softly. 'Come here, boy.' Walking behind her, Jago held the lamp high, casting as much light around them as possible. He did not shout, fearing a strange voice might cause the dog to run. After about five minutes, when there was still no sign of the hound, her voice took an anxious turn.

'Might I make a suggestion, Miss Shackleford,' he said at length. Clearly startled at the sudden sound of his voice, she turned quickly and abruptly lost her balance. With a gasp, she fell towards him, her arms pinwheeling in an effort to remain upright. Hampered by concern for the oil lamp in his hand, Jago reached out awkwardly with his free arm to slow her fall. Unfortunately, the only part of her person his hand connected with was her bosom. He just had time to register the enticing feel of her curves, when she drew back her hand and gave him a resounding slap on the face. With an oath, he pulled his hand back and with a small shriek she continued her fall, twisting at the last minute and succeeding in head butting his nose. With a pained grunt, Jago fell backwards, landing on his arse with

Charity Shackleford seated in his lap. Seconds later, the lamp went out.

There was a frozen silence. Absurdly, Jago felt parts of him that hadn't seen light in months begin to stir at the feeling of her backside against his crotch, until the sting of his cheek and the pain in his nose brought him crashing back down to earth. It was pitch black, and he felt his burden begin to tremble. Swearing internally, he opened his mouth to ask if she was hurt when he abruptly realised she was *laughing*. But before he had time to process such an unexpected development, a sudden crashing in the undergrowth signalled the arrival of something large. Seconds later, they were set upon by a large furry beast. It was Freddy. Clearly none the worse from his culinary adventures.

∞∞∞

Pulling the threadbare covers up to his chin, Percy shivered in the damp cold of his lodging house and thought about his predicament. No matter which way he looked at it, his first duty was to save his mother's immortal soul. Naturally, ensuring her release from the dingy cell she was currently residing in was a close second. And Percy had no idea how he was going to do either.

He wasn't accustomed to dealing with such complex problems. At least not unaided. He thought back to the letter he'd left for the Reverend, already regretting his written avowal that this was something he had to do alone. What on earth had he been thinking?

Confessing to the Reverend that his mother was involved in smuggling was not at all the same as admitting it to the Duke of Blackmore. And anyway, it was more than likely his superior already knew, given the quality of the brandy they both enjoyed during most evenings. Percy squeezed his eyes shut, wondering if his mother's arrest was the Lord's way of punishing him for not speaking out. Ignoring his mother's clandestine activities and the Reverend's suspected involvement was every bit as bad as pardoning them.

But shockingly, at this moment, Percy didn't care a jot whether Augustus Shackleford was complicit in Mary Noon's illegal dealings, he just wished the Reverend was here to tell him what to do…

∞∞∞

It was midnight by the time their carriage drew up outside the Castle Inn. Of the three of them, Freddy was definitely the sprightliest. Whatever he'd eaten had certainly not kept the hound down for long. Both the Reverend and Charity on the other hand looked as though they'd been dug up, as Prudence would no doubt have observed.

Clutching Freddy's lead tightly, Charity winced as she climbed down from the carriage. It felt as though every bone hurt. As she waited for her father to descend, her thoughts inevitably went back to the earlier search for their errant hound. And more specifically, Mr Jago Cardell.

She knew nothing about him except that he was tall. She hadn't even been able to see him clearly in the darkness, so could only guess at his looks. Nevertheless, there had been something intriguing about him. Her face flamed again as she thought back to the compromising position they'd finished up in. What the deuce must he have thought of her? Especially her wholly inappropriate laughter. In truth, her mirth had been more than a little hysterical, though she wasn't usually given to such histrionics.

Determinedly, she put the matter aside. She was very unlikely to see the man again, and for now, she needed to focus on helping her father rescue Mary Noon. Guilty the woman may be, but she was also Percy's mother, and the whole Shackleford family owed the curate more than any of them could ever repay - even if much of their gratitude was for Percy's oft futile attempts to keep their father out of mischief.

After the carriage and horses had been led away by the stable hands, Charity and the Reverend were fortunate enough to be given their own small but pleasantly furnished rooms. On entering the chamber,

Charity wearily unfastened her cloak, while a maid bustled about, stoking up the fire in the hearth and placing a warming pan into the bed.

As soon as the maid left, Charity undressed and climbed gratefully into bed. Within minutes she was sound asleep.

CHAPTER 5

'You reckon on leavin' 'er to rot then, Jack? I mean wot if she squeals?'

'Mary knows better than that. If she so much as opens her mouth, she'll end up in one of those barrels.' The leader of the Hope Cove gang of smugglers, simply known as Jack, nodded towards the casks of brandy being dragged to the surface. Twenty in all, they'd been brought in over a week earlier and lashed together with weights to hide them from the revenue men. Once hauled off the beach, the contraband would be taken half a mile inland and hidden underneath the cellar of the Kings Arms.

Glancing back, Jack could just make out the twelve broad-shouldered tubmen on the edge of the beach, each with a pair of wooden half-ankers at his feet, ready and waiting to carry the spirits to their initial destination.

'So what did our friend Cardell have to say?' Jack continued, his eyes carefully scanning the cliffs surrounding the secluded cove they were in.

'Reckons 'e knows summat, but wants in afore he spills 'is guts. Says he'll only speak to you.'

Jack looked over at the wiry man next to him. 'Tell Flynn to deal with it. I want to know what Cardell knows. He gives it first, then we'll talk. If he refuses, tell Flynn to beat it out of him, then slit his bloody throat and send him to the locker.'

∞∞∞

Despite her exhaustion, Charity woke up early the next morning, her first thoughts of her twin. By now, she and Grace would have arrived in Torquay. Charity envied them the time they would get to spend with Faith but understood Grace's reasoning for not taking them both to Redstone House.

Leaving the Reverend to his own devices was simply not an option, and though it had been Chastity who'd needed removing from Blackmore, sending her to assist their father would be akin to throwing the tinder box into the fire. Even when Grace had believed him simply attending a deathbed.

Sighing, Charity pushed aside the coverlet, shivering at the chill. Wondering at the time, she went to the window and peeped through the drapes. Dawn was still an hour or more away, far too early for the maid to remake the fire. Pressing her nose against the glass, Charity peered down to the courtyard below. Flickering candles casting fanciful shadows around the yard gave evidence that despite the early hour, not everyone was still abed.

Wrapping herself in a blanket, Charity carefully made her way towards the fireplace, the slight glow of last night's embers her only light. Crouching down in front of the hearth, she picked up the poker and stirred at the embers in the grate. Fortunately, there was still enough heat, and after a few moments, she carefully added more coal from the basket before sitting back on her heels to wait for it to catch.

As the fire began to light up the room, Charity glanced about and observing the outline of two candlesticks positioned by the bed, she climbed to her feet. Picking one up, she took it back to the fire and carefully holding out the end of the candle to the small flame, she managed to light the wick. Had Grace been present, she would no doubt have rung a fine peal over her head for taking such a risk.

Placing the candlestick onto the small bedside table, Charity picked up her book and was preparing to climb back into bed when, all of a sudden, she heard footsteps. Frowning, she paused, remembering she and her father had the only two rooms at the top of the inn. Abruptly wondering if her father could be in trouble, she scooted backwards off the bed and ran towards the door. Pulling it ajar, she stuck her head out, just in time to see her father start down the narrow stairs. The light from the candle in his hand revealed him to be fully dressed, and though she could only see his back as he carefully descended, it was clear Freddy wasn't with him. A feeling of dread shot through her. Where the deuce was he going? Clearly not to take Freddy out to do his business.

She quietly closed the door and stood still for a second. There was no way she could simply return to bed now. Hastily, she pulled on her dress and cloak and pushed her bare feet into her half boots. Without any stockings, they were hard to pull on and she wasted valuable seconds trying to shove her feet into the freezing cold leather. Finally, pulling open the door onto the landing, she was frustrated to see it back to darkness. Any light shed by her father's candle had completely disappeared, and she had no idea where he could have gone.

Resisting the urge to stamp her feet in vexation, she hesitated on the threshold. She would be foolhardy indeed to go wandering about the inn aimlessly. What was her father doing, and why hadn't he taken Freddy? A sudden idea took hold, and before she had the chance to question whether she'd possibly taken leave of her senses, she quickly went to fetch the candlestick and stepped out onto the small landing, pulling her door shut behind her.

Seconds later, she pushed open the door to her father's room where the foxhound looked up sleepily. 'Good boy, Freddy,' she whispered, stepping inside and holding her candle high to look for his lead. Once secured, she pulled the reluctant hound off the bed. The disgruntled look he gave her spoke volumes. Clearly, he thought her completely addled.

'You may be right, boy,' she muttered, looking for something of her father's she could use. Finally, coming upon a reasonably clean handkerchief, she grimaced slightly, then held it to Freddy's nose. 'Find,' she whispered. The foxhound yawned, then looked up at her. For a second, she thought he was going to ignore her instruction – it wouldn't have been the first time - but after a few seconds, he sniffed at the square of linen again and trotted to the door.

Holding his lead tightly in one hand and the candlestick in the other, she followed Freddy down the stairs, taking care not to trip over her dress. On the landing below theirs, the foxhound stopped and lifted his head while she stared apprehensively into the shrouded darkness of a narrow corridor. After nearly half a minute when she thought her heart likely to burst through her chest, he put his head back down to the floor and continued to the top of the next set of stairs which were fortunately much wider.

Freddy didn't lift his head again until they reached the public areas of the inn, where, to her horror, he went straight to the front door, looking back at her expectantly. Charity could feel the cold flagstones through her thin boots. Stupidly, when she'd returned for the candle in her bedchamber, she'd forgotten to put on her stockings.

If her father had ventured outside the inn, she couldn't possibly think to follow him. Feeling sick, she lingered uncertainly at the door. This was foolish in the extreme. She should return post-haste to her bedchamber.

She'd just taken a hesitant step back towards the stairs, when she suddenly heard voices. Panicking, she glanced wildly about, finally spying another door to her left. Hurriedly she ran towards it, dragging the reluctant foxhound behind her. Fortunately, the door wasn't locked, and pushing it open hastily she slipped inside. After coaxing Freddy through the opening, she pushed the door shut and looked around.

She was in what looked like a small office, fortunately unoccupied. Ignoring her thudding heart, she put the candlestick on a low table well away from the door to prevent any light from showing, then went back to listen.

Looking down at Freddy, she put her fingers to her lips in a shushing motion, whispering 'Quiet boy,' before carefully opening the door slightly to peer through the crack.

At first, everything was dark, and she could no longer hear the voices. But gradually, a light began to appear, revealing a narrow corridor she'd previously missed. She watched as one light became two, bobbing up and down, getting steadily closer until the shadowy shapes in the hall became pieces of furniture. Hardly daring to breathe, she waited.

'This ain't safe, Jack. There be too many bodies stayin' 'ere. We'll all of us be heading for the bloody mornin' drop if it goes on.'

'You won't live long enough to swing if you don't stop your blabber.' The nonchalant manner in which the threat was offered made the words all the more chilling, and unaccountably, the hairs on Charity's arms stood on end in response. Freddy obviously felt it too as his hackles rose, and he gave a low, warning growl.

Hurriedly, Charity crouched down and pulled Freddy to her, burying the foxhound's nose into her cloak and stroking his furry ears with gentle but urgent fingers. When the hound subsided, she climbed to her feet once more, inexplicably anxious to see the owner of the chilling voice. Holding on to Freddy's collar, she put her eye back to the gap in the door.

The two men had reached the hall. The innkeeper she'd met the night before, and his wringing hands, confirmed he wasn't the one issuing the warning. The man named Jack was tall and lean, with long, unkempt hair. His face, highlighted by the candle in his hand, was ordinary in the extreme. But something in the man's gaze turned Charity's blood to ice.

'So when's the next crop?' the innkeeper was asking, in a much more subdued tone.

'I'll be in tou...' Just then, Freddy let out another low growl. Jack instantly stopped and stared in the direction of the office. Smothering a frightened whimper, Charity crouched down again and shushed the anxious foxhound. Squeezing her eyes shut, she remained utterly still, her head covering Freddy's. The only other time she'd been this terrified was when Anthony nearly drowned in Wistman's pool.

The silence in the hall seemed to go on forever, but at length, the man spoke again, his voice as emotionless as before. 'I suggest you keep that mongrel of yours quiet, Charlie, or next time, I'll slit its bloody throat.'

The innkeeper mumbled something, but whatever he said was inaudible over the abrupt sound of footsteps on the flagstones. As the feet approached her hiding place, she put her hand over Freddy's muzzle, choking back tears of fright, but to her relief, the footsteps continued past, and a few seconds later, she heard the front door open and close.

Despite the sound of the innkeeper retreating in the other direction, Charity remained where she was for a full five minutes after the last glimmer of candlelight had vanished from the crack in the door. Finally climbing to her feet, she determinedly swallowed her fear and cautiously peeped around the door, then confirming the hall was empty, she grabbed hold of her candlestick and fled upstairs to her bedchamber.

∞∞∞

'*Charity*. Are you in there girl? Some varmint's made off with Freddy.' It was the frantic knocking accompanying her father's shouts that finally woke her. Blearily, Charity turned over and found herself nose to nose with … Freddy. What…? She struggled to a sitting position, which wasn't easy with a two and a half stone bundle of fur holding down the bedclothes, and clearly Freddy had no intention of moving anytime soon. Charity gave a small groan as her memory of earlier came crashing back.

'For pity's sake, come in, Father,' she yelled as the pounding began reverberating inside her head.

Flinging open the door, the Reverend stomped in, a picture of panic, only to stop short when he saw the foxhound comfortably curled up on his daughter's bed.

'What the deuce are you doing with Freddy?' he demanded.

'What the deuce were you doing sneaking around before dawn?' she countered waspishly.

Her question put an abrupt end to the Reverend's tirade as he opened his mouth, then shut it again.

'If you would be good enough to remove yourself from my bedchamber, Father,' Charity continued tartly, 'I will get dressed and meet you downstairs. Naturally, I am waiting with bated breath to discover where you disappeared to this morning. As I am sure is Freddy.'

She looked over at the comatose foxhound who was doing a very good job of masking his excitement. 'Perhaps we may discuss it further over some breakfast?'

The Reverend looked as though he'd rather break his fast with old Nick himself, but he said nothing, simply hmphed and retreated, calling to Freddy before hastily shutting the door.

Sighing, Charity climbed out of bed for the second time that day.

CHAPTER 6

The rain in the night had turned the narrower streets of Dartmouth to mush, and Jago found himself swearing out loud as he attempted to navigate round the larger water-filled holes.

There was no getting around it, yesterday had been a disaster. Just when he'd thought he was getting close to identifying the mysterious Jack. He sighed in frustration. If the smugglers' leader didn't take the bait...? Well, in truth, he'd run out of ideas.

And more than that, he was done to a cow's thumb. He'd been tracking the man he believed killed his sister for nigh on two years. First to Kingsbridge and Salcombe. Eighteen months working with the local fishermen in Salcombe while slowly integrating himself into the small smuggling community that operated around the Kingsbridge estuary. It had taken the best part of a year before he'd been trusted enough to take part in the runs and nearly another six before the name *Jack* was mentioned.

Slowly, he'd learned that the men he ran with were small fry. For the most part, they were simple fishermen supplementing their income as free traders. They kept well clear of the larger, more organised gangs to the east. More organised and infinitely more vicious, comprising men who thought nothing of throwing innocent people off a cliff to protect their anonymity.

The most notorious of these was the Hope Cove gang led by the man who called himself Jack. No one seemed to know what his real name was or even what he looked like. He was just a ghost, a bogeyman to frighten children with. The gang operated all the way from Seaton in East Devon to Falmouth in Cornwall. With only a handful of Customs officers operating out of Dartmouth and Plymouth, they were able to ply their illegal trade almost unchallenged.

Then three months ago, Jago heard a rumour that the elusive Jack operated from Dartmouth. According to the inebriated fisherman who'd shared the tale, Jack apparently enjoyed the challenge of bamboozling the authorities.

The other fishermen had declared the tale a bag o' bloody moonshine, but Jago could hear the fear behind their jeering denunciation.

Over the next couple of months, Jago had discreetly let it be known he'd be interested in joining the Hope Cove gang, but though his cohorts had professed him bloody addled, he hadn't been approached.

In the end, he'd packed his bags and walked the twenty-three-mile coast path from Salcombe to Dartmouth, taking a labouring job unloading legitimate cargo in the bustling harbour. It was back-breaking work, but Jago had really believed he was finally getting closer to infiltrating the notorious smuggling ring.

Unfortunately, last night, it became evident that Jack had little interest in any supposed information he might possess, and even less in recruiting him. More than that, he'd been warned off.

Jago swore as he approached the wharf. Time was running out. He couldn't stay away from Wheal Tredennick indefinitely. Leaving the mine in the hands of his shattered, embittered father would eventually lead them to ruin. He needed to finish this business and swiftly.

∞∞∞∞

'Thunder an' turf, Freddy lad,' Reverend Shackleford muttered as he watched the hound cock his leg up over something unpleasant in the alley behind the inn. 'You'd think after six virtually unmanageable daughters, the Almighty would have graced me with at least one obedient offspring.' Freddy looked up and wagged his tail, and while the foxhound's response didn't provide quite the same comfort as Percy's would no doubt have done, the Reverend chose to take it as agreement.

Sighing, Augustus Shackleford headed back into the inn's small front parlour where Charity was already waiting for him, feet tapping impatiently, a tray of bread and butter on the table in front of her.

'So, what have you got to say for yourself, Father?' Charity demanded as soon as he'd sat down.

'Have you ordered tea,' the Reverend responded, clearly stalling for time. Charity pursed her lips and nodded her head. In truth, the fright she'd had in the early hours had made her much angrier with her father than she would have been ordinarily. It wasn't often Charity felt out of her depth, but cowering in the inn's small office, she'd felt a totally unfamiliar sense of dread.

To Reverend Shackleford's relief, the maid chose that moment to come over with two dishes of tea and some preserves, giving him a brief reprieve. Unfortunately, it only lasted until he'd taken the first bite. At Charity's frosty glare, he finally sighed and put his piece of bread back onto its plate.

'I was worried about Percy,' he said with a self-conscious scowl. 'The thought of him wandering about in ... well, anywhere other than Blackmore...' he paused and grimaced. 'The chucklehead could end up being deported.'

'From Dartmouth?' Charity questioned incredulously. 'I think you do him a disservice, Father. Percy has more sense than you give him credit for.'

'You don't know him like I do,' grumbled the Reverend. 'He isn't accustomed to doing things without my guidance.'

Charity gave a rude snort, but all she said was, 'Why the devil were you looking for him in the middle of the night?'

'Couldn't sleep. And it wasn't the middle of the night. I am after all in the service of the Church and am accustomed to getting up for matins,' her father declared piously.

'Three times a year,' scoffed Charity. 'And what would have happened if you'd been attacked? You could still be lying in a gutter somewhere.'

'Not many will risk the slippery slope downstairs by attacking a man of the cloth,' the Reverend responded tapping his nose and giving a knowing nod towards the floor.

Charity gave another snort. Nevertheless, she was mollified somewhat. Her father's concern for his curate was commendable. 'You should have taken Freddy,' she remarked instead, helping herself to a piece of bread. 'You'd have found Percy by now if you'd used his nose.'

'I was more concerned about the noise he'd make,' the Reverend confessed. 'Trusting Freddy's nose in Blackmore is one thing. 'Relying on it in a strange town…' He paused and shuddered, before adding, 'We could have ended up in the deuced river. And anyway what was he doing in your bedchamber?'

Charity liberally spread her piece of bread with butter and blackcurrant preserve before answering. In truth, she wasn't entirely sure what to say. To accuse the innkeeper of being involved in smuggling activities – well, it certainly wouldn't help Mary Noon's cause.

That said, her instincts told her the man he called Jack was both dangerous and cruel. The casual way he'd spoken about cutting the dog's throat. Charity felt again the inexplicable surge of pure dread she'd felt when spying on him. The man was evil, of that she was certain. It would be much better if he did not come to her father's attention or, more importantly, her father did not come to his.

'I thought to use Freddy to see where you had gone,' she said cagily, biting into her bread and chewing it hurriedly. 'Indeed, he followed the scent from your handkerchief with no uncertainty, taking me straight to the front door.'

'Tare an' hounds, girl, don't tell me you were wandering the streets of Dartmouth in the early hours.' The horror in his voice warmed her until he added, 'It's going to nigh on clean me out to get Percy's mother freed. Having you added to the mix would have deuced well put me in Dun territory.'

'Your concern for my welfare is heartening, Father,' she retorted, 'I have much more common sense than to negotiate the streets of Dartmouth in the dark.' She paused and narrowed her eyes before adding, 'And I'm entirely certain you have no intention of buying Mrs Noon's freedom.'

Her father hmphed and helped himself to more tea. 'Still, using Freddy to find Percy during daylight will not be quite so likely to land us in a hobble,' he mused, seconds later.

'Why can't we just wait for him at the gaol?' Charity queried. 'Percy will undoubtedly turn up if he wishes to see his mother released.'

'That may be the case,' her father acknowledged, 'but knowing Percy, he could end up in the basket well before he even gets to the gaol.'

'That only usually happens when he's with you, Father,' Charity countered, pushing her chair back. 'Do you have anything of Percy's you could give Freddy to sniff?'

Reverend Shackleford climbed to his feet with a frown. 'Only the letter he left for me.'

'Well that should be sufficient,' Charity approved with a nod, picking up her gloves. 'While you go to fetch the letter, I think I'll walk down to the quayside. I'll take Freddy,' she added, when her father opened his mouth to object. 'I suggest we meet by the river in fifteen minutes.' With that, she put on her gloves, picked up Freddy's lead and swept out of the room, leaving her father muttering about deuced bossy daughters.

Charity picked her way through the muddied roads towards the river, enjoying the hustle and bustle of the busy town. The scent of fresh bread vied with the detritus littering the paths and the stench of fish. And over it all, the smell of the sea. Freddy especially enjoyed the variety of odours, and when not nosing in the filth on the ground, held his nose high in the air sniffing excitedly. Accustomed to the mostly wholesome smells of the countryside, Charity initially found the concoction of aromas almost too much. It was entirely different to Torquay, the only other seaside town she'd visited, which was much more genteel.

But with so much to look at, she soon forgot about the stink. Everywhere there was a sense of aliveness, of exhilaration, of endless possibilities. It was from here the Mayflower had first set sail for the Americas.

As she approached the river, Charity stopped short at the sight of two large merchant ships, their cargo being offloaded by a gang of brawny men, shouting and even laughing as they heaved the goods on their backs. She wondered if any of the vessels had been victims of smugglers. Or had they willingly shared a portion of their cargo? Taking care not to get too close, she watched as casks of liquor were hauled ashore. Was it from a ship like this that Mary Noon had pilfered her brandy?

Hearing footsteps behind her, she turned to find her father hurrying towards her, waving Percy's letter triumphantly in the air. 'Gadzooks, I'm not accustomed to such exercise so early in the day,' he puffed as he reached her.

'Would you like to sit down for a moment?' Charity asked, eying his red face. The Reverend gave her an irritable glance. 'I'm not ready for me reward just yet,' he grumbled. In answer, she simply handed over Freddy's lead with a sigh.

'Right then, Freddy lad. This is a chance to redeem yourself after that debacle last night.' He held out the paper for the foxhound to sniff. Freddy's tail began wagging, and he licked the sheet, obviously getting a whiff of his favourite person. The Reverend nodded in satisfaction. 'Find Percy, Freddy,' he ordered. When the dog didn't move, he added a hopeful, 'Good boy.'

The foxhound gave the paper another sniff, then abruptly took off in the direction of the smaller fishing boats moored further up the river.

'Tare an' hou...,' Reverend Shackleford yelped as the lead abruptly jerked his arm forward, dragging him after the dog.

'Don't let him go, Father,' Charity yelled, picking up her skirts and giving chase.

Reverend Shackleford didn't answer, being occupied with other things. 'Freddy, *slow*,' he bellowed after being nearly yanked off his feet for the third time. But either the foxhound was too focused on finding his adored provider of Mrs Tomlinson's bread and butter pudding to listen, or he was simply turning a deaf ear. Probably both.

Seconds later, they reached the first of the fishing boats. At this point, Mrs Tomlinson's bread and butter pudding most definitely took a back seat to the large barrel of fish guts Freddy had just spied.

Jumping up ecstatically, the foxhound managed to push over the cask, allowing the stinking mess to pool onto the ground.

Then, ignoring the 'Oy, what you think you're doin'', coming from the fishing boat, he leapt over the fallen barrel, straight into the mess on the other side.

Belatedly, the Reverend let go of the lead, but unfortunately, Freddy's flying leap had started the barrel rolling towards the oncoming clergyman. With a whoomph, Augustus Shackleford tripped and fell forward, his body sprawled over the barrel which was now rolling back the other way.

With a gasp, Charity stopped and put her hand up to her mouth as she watched her father topple with agonising slowness headfirst into the pile of fish guts. After a second, fighting an insane desire to laugh, she picked up her skirts and hurried to see if he needed help.

Just as a familiar voice piped up, 'What on earth are you doing, Sir? I didn't know you were in Dartmouth.'

'Don't just deuced well stand there, Percy, come over here and give me a hand.'

CHAPTER 7

An hour later, they were sitting in a cosy coffee house aptly named the Fisherman's Rest which meant the faint whiff clinging to Reverend Shackleford's second best cassock was not remarked upon. That said, the clergyman had plenty to say on the subject of disobedient dogs and the cost of having his best cassock laundered.

'Well, he did find Percy,' reasoned Charity.

'And I have to say I am exceeding glad to see you, Sir,' the curate added fervently.

'Have you seen your mother, Percy?' Charity asked.

'I haven't … I didn't …,' the small man muttered, looking as though he was about to burst into tears.

The Reverend sighed and patted Percy on the back. 'That's what we're here for, lad,' he reassured his curate. 'As soon as we've finished here, we'll go directly to the gaol.'

Their conversation was interrupted by a sudden loud whine from outside the coffee house where Freddy had been tied up to contemplate the error of his ways. Of course, there was also the hope that the fresh sea air might deaden the smell of rotting fish that clung stubbornly to his muzzle. In truth, the foxhound didn't appear to be doing much contemplating and was peering through the window, his nose pressed to the glass.

Charity, who was facing towards the front windows of the coffee house, suddenly gave a small gasp as she saw a tall man walk past the hound, before abruptly stopping and turning back. 'Hello, boy,' she heard him say faintly, bending down. Watching, she saw the moment he recoiled slightly as the stench hit him, muttering, 'No wonder they've left you out here. Have you been up to mischief again?' Standing back up, their would-be rescuer from last night stared in through the window.

Charity fought the urge to duck. Mayhap Mr Cardell would not recognise her in the daylight. Though as she stared at his swarthy countenance, she was suddenly convinced she would have recognised him anywhere. She knew the moment he identified her, and the expression on his face set her heart thudding. Surprise, coupled with something else. A wariness bordering on fear. Confused, Charity looked back down at her tea. She might have made a bit of a cake of herself last evening, but there was certainly no reason for him to look at her so. She kept her eyes down, expecting him to simply walk on, but instead, a small bell rang as the door was pushed open.

Seconds later, he was at their table. 'Miss Shackleford, Reverend Shackleford, how pleasant to see you again,' he murmured with a bend of his head. 'I trust you've suffered no ill effects from our misadventure last night.' He nodded towards the window and the disgraced foxhound, adding with a small grin, 'I see Freddy has been up to more mischief.'

Surprised he'd remembered the dog's name, Charity looked up, and her eyes widened. Looming over her, Jago Cardell was ... well, *enormous*. How had she failed to notice this last night? He was at least six foot four with muscular forearms and hands the size of small dinner plates. She found herself remembering their mishap last night, and abruptly wondered how it would feel to be entirely enfolded in his large arms, immediately feeling flustered at the thought.

'Mr Cardell,' her father was saying jovially. 'This is certainly a fortuitous meeting. Might I purchase you a hot beverage in thanks for your timely assistance last night?'

'Unfortunately, my shift in the boatyard begins in ten minutes, and they do not take kindly to laggards.' Jago excused himself with a rueful smile.

Charity continued to stare up at him curiously. His attire was that of a working man, but both his voice and manner were more reminiscent of a gentleman.

'Mayhap you would care to join us this evening for a meal, Mr Cardell,' she found herself saying, even as she wondered at her temerity. He looked directly at her for the first time, and she drew in her breath. His eyes were the colour of dark honey and fringed with long black lashes. He stared down at her for a second as if uncertain how to answer, then he gave a short bow.

'I should be honoured, Miss Shackleford. My shift finishes at dusk.'

'Excellent,' Reverend Shackleford interjected. 'We are staying in the Castle Inn, Mr Cardell. We will await you in the bar.' He turned towards Percy who had remained uncomfortably silent during the exchange. 'This is my curate, Mr Percy Noon. He will be joining us for dinner this evening.' Percy gave a startled glance towards the Reverend.

'Oh, I'm not entir…'

'Is eight p.m. agreeable?' Augustus Shackleford interjected before Percy had the chance to launch into a lengthy list of excuses.

Jago inclined his head towards the curate, then turned back to the

Reverend. 'I shall look forward to it.' He gave a slow smile which did peculiar things to Charity's insides.

'They have an excellent menu I believe,' she gushed.

She actually *gushed*. Good grief she was turning into Chastity. Mortified, she looked down at her hands, helpless to stop her face reddening. A few minutes later, to her relief, he took his leave.

'Do you think it a good idea to broadcast our presence here, Sir?' Percy cautioned.

'Mr Cardell may be able to further our cause,' responded the Reverend, dismissing his curate's concerns. 'After all, it is likely he knows people that we do not.' He swallowed the last of his tea.

'Come then, it's time we visited Mary to see how the land lies, if we wish to put this whole havey-cavey business to bed. After all, we don't wish to be lingering in Dartmouth for any longer than necessary. Agnes will have my proverbials if I'm not returned by the time her salts run out.'

∞∞∞

Jago roundly cursed himself as he made his way towards the docks. What the devil had he been thinking to accept such an invitation? To blasted dinner of all things. Was he so desperate for the company of a pretty face that he'd risk everything? If anyone connected to the smuggling ring happened to spy him enjoying dinner with strangers, it would likely provoke their suspicions and almost certainly scupper any chance of him learning the identity of the elusive Jack, however remote that might seem at the moment. He would have to cancel.

His mind made up, he tried to put the matter aside as he made his way along the waterfront to the first of the merchant ships alongside. Unfortunately, Charity Shackleford's face would not be so easily banished. He remembered the feel of her pressing against his baubles and ridiculously, he felt himself stir.

Bloody hell, he was acting like a green lad. At nine and twenty he should know better. True, it was nearly three years since he'd last lost himself in the softness of a woman's body, but he could not afford to be distracted after so long. Obtaining justice for his sister was the only thing that mattered.

∞∞∞

The Dartmouth gaol was situated surprisingly close to the Castle Inn, on Hanover place. Indeed, Reverend Shackleford found it slightly alarming to realise he'd been sleeping not more than fifty yards away from potential gallows birds. However, he drew some comfort from the fact that the gaol was actually only steps away from St. Saviour's Church, and since the Almighty was well aware that they were on a mission of mercy, the Reverend was (almost) entirely certain that no harm would come to them from their close proximity to any varlets that might currently be languishing behind bars.

Fortunately, the only *varlet* locked up at that particular moment in time turned out to be Percy's mother. In truth, Dartmouth's only gaol turned out to be a bit of an anti-climax.

Consisting of two vaulted rooms, the smell of which assaulted their noses a good few feet away, the sole guard - if the slovenly individual could be referred to as such - was sitting on the step outside eating a hunk of bread and cheese.

'I wish to speak with your prisoner,' Reverend Shackleford demanded in the doom-laden voice he usually reserved for his more reluctant parishioners.

'Wot yer want 'er for?' was his shrugged response. 'You thinkin' to save her, revren?' He laughed loudly, slapping his thigh. 'Even if she escapes the mornin' drop, there ain't no way that bloody harridan's gettin' through the pearly gates.'

'Blast and bugger yer eyes, Joseph Smith. If I'm 'eadin' downstairs, you'll be right behind me, yer bloody old goat,' came a loud female voice from inside, followed by an ear-splitting cackle.

The indelicate voice clearly belonged to his mother, if Percy's pained expression was anything to go by.

'Oh bloody stubble it, you bracket-faced old trollop,' the guard grumbled, clearly losing interest in baiting his prisoner.

Percy drew himself up indignantly. 'I'll have you know that's my mo…' he began, only to be interrupted by the Reverend's next words. 'I'm certain you're beyond thankful that saving Mrs Noon's immortal soul is not your responsibility, my good man, but mayhap a little more attention to your own hereafter would not go amiss. After all, we are any of us only here by God's grace.'

Charity stared over at her father as the guard blanched slightly. Sometimes she forgot that he was actually quite good at being a cleric.

Shrugging, the guard went back to his bread and cheese. 'Yer welcome to 'er,' was all he muttered, with a nod towards the entrance.

'Right then, Percy, we'll give you a couple of minutes to get said what you need to, then we'll come in.'

'I don't think I'm even going to need a couple of seconds, Sir. Our relationship…' He paused before finishing with a grimace, 'We are not close.'

'Now there's a surprise,' sighed the Reverend. 'Lead on then, lad, and let's get this bag of moonshine sorted once and for all.'

The inside of the gaol was dark and murky, the only illumination coming from a tallow candle that was giving off more smoke than light. The smell also increased tenfold, and with a cough, Charity put her handkerchief over her nose. Freddy, his tail tucked between his legs, whimpered slightly. Clearly, he preferred the smell of rotten fish.

'Bit delicate, are we?' A low chortle accompanied her words and lifting her kerchief away, Charity looked over at the woman who was evidently Percy's mother. Thin and angular like her son, Mary Noon was clothed in what looked like it may once have been a day dress, now ripped and soiled beyond repair. Her hair hung around her face in greasy grey strands, and her face was so dirty, it was difficult to guess what she actually looked like.

Percy seemed to have lost the use of his tongue, but the horrified look on his face spoke volumes.

'Hello, Mary…' began Reverend Shackleford.

'Don't you *'ello* me, you whey-face bag o' bloody wind, Augustus Shackleford. It's taken you bloody long enough to get 'ere.'

'Well, better late than never,' the Reverend defended, clearly struggling to remain civil. 'We're here to help you get out of this cell.'

Mary Noon gave a loud guffaw. 'Yer mean yer not 'ere to make sure the bloody Gobblers ain't taken the bottle o' brandy wi' your name on it?'

Reverend Shackleford winced. Clearly, the thought had crossed his mind. He opened his mouth to speak, but Mary got there first. 'An, anyway, owd yer know I be wantin' to leave?'

'Surely, you can't wish to stay locked up in such a … horrible place?' Charity burst out.

Percy's mother gave a low chortle. 'I'm safer in 'ere than out there. Less likely to end up in the bleedin' river wi' a rock tied to me foot.'

'But what if they decide to hang you, Mother,' Percy protested, speaking for the first time. Mary Noon turned towards her son, and Charity thought she saw a faint softening in her expression. 'They ain't goin' to crop me,' she scoffed. 'I'm more useful to 'em sat in 'ere.' She grinned. 'An' I get me three square meals wi' out havin' to stump up any blunt.'

'Why are you so afraid to leave?' Charity asked, sensing real fear underneath Mary's brevity. 'Do you know something you shouldn't?'

Percy's mother looked over at her shrewdly. 'Well ain't you the clever one,' she muttered. 'I know lots o' things I shouldn't.' She tapped the side of her nose. 'Happy Jack reckons I'm too ripe and ready by bloody 'alf. He'd like to see me gone an' 'e don't care 'ow it's done.'

'*Jack*,' Charity interrupted, remembering that was the name given to the terrifying man speaking with the innkeeper. 'Is he a … a … free trader?'

'E's a bastard is wot 'e is,' was all Mary answered, spitting on the ground for good measure. But for the first time, her fear showed.

'Wha … what does he look like?' Charity asked.

'I'd be shoutin' it from the bloody rooftops if I knew,' Mary snapped. 'Ain't never seen 'im, an' don't know anyone who 'as. Or at least they ain't sayin.' Charity felt her heart begin to thump erratically, but before she could say anything, Percy blurted, 'We have to get you out of here, Mother.'

'I aint leavin' until I got somewhere safe to go,' Mary Noon shrugged. 'If I go back 'ome, it's only a matter o' time afore I'm pushing up bloody daisies.'

'What if we find you somewhere to hide?' Reverend Shackleford questioned a little desperately. 'Will you allow us to buy your freedom then?'

Mary Noon snorted. 'Buy my freedom? I'd be out afore you could say piss off if I wanted. Bleedin' Gobblers know I'm too scared to run. Put yer blunt away. Just find me somewhere to go where I ain't likely to end up in Davy Jones' Locker.'

CHAPTER 8

It was late afternoon, and the Reverend was sitting alone in the main bar at the Castle Inn. Charity had retired to her room for a rest before dinner, and Percy had gone to remove his belongings from his miserable lodging rooms.

Augustus Shackleford took a long sip of his tankard of ale and sighed. How had everything become so deuced complicated? From merely expecting to effect Mary Noon's freedom by greasing a few palms, they'd suddenly landed in the middle of some decidedly havey-cavey business. He'd always believed Percy's mother to be of little consequence to the smuggling gangs around Salcombe. That she was simply helping the free traders out now and then to supplement the pittance she lived on. But if what she'd hinted was true, she was much more involved than she'd previously let on.

Reverend Shackleford didn't think she was telling a plumper – the fear on her face was too real for that - and she definitely wasn't dicked in the nob, whatever Percy preferred to believe. He took another sip of his ale. The knowledge that he'd potentially been aiding and abetting ark ruffians by purchasing illicit brandy didn't sit well at all, even if it was only a few bottles a year.

Unquestionably, it was his duty to see to the safety of Percy's mother, but he had no idea where he was going to stash such a foul-mouthed harridan. Obviously, he couldn't take her back to Blackmore. Agnes would have an apoplexy, and goodness knows what Nicholas would have to say about the matter. And that was without considering the danger he could be putting them all in if this *Jack* got wind of her hiding place.

And to top it all, he'd involved his daughter in the whole smoky business.

The Reverend felt like crying. He had no idea what to do and couldn't remember the last time he'd been so bereft of ideas.

He took another sip of his ale. Mayhap he was in need of some sustenance. He nodded his head in satisfaction. That was it. He was certain some cold meats and cheeses would help with the thinking process. Along with another tankard of ale naturally…

∞∞∞

Charity lay on her bed trying to sleep. But try as she might, she could not seem to stop the thoughts from chasing around her head.

Mary Noon was in terrible trouble. That much was abundantly clear. Clearly, the Customs Officers had no interest in what happened to her unless she gave them something useful, and Charity suspected that while her confession might see the arrest of several members of the smuggling ring, their leader would walk away scot-free. And of course Mary herself would be unlikely to live long enough to celebrate her freedom.

Sighing, she turned over and cuddled Freddy who was snoring loudly next to her. He'd been scrubbed with water and sand on their return to their accommodation, then rubbed down with strewing herbs. The whole procedure another cost her father had been none too happy about. But now, though still damp, the foxhound was smelling much sweeter.

Mary did not know what Jack looked like. But Charity did. Would it help if she informed the authorities that she'd seen the face of the notorious leader of the Hope Cove gang? Or would she simply be consigning herself to the same watery grave Percy's mother feared?

Her thoughts turned to Jago Cardell. Mayhap he *would* be able to help them as her father had hinted. But then, he could be one of the smugglers himself. Charity frowned. Somehow, she didn't think so. While she didn't know him at all, she felt deep inside that there was something honest about him. His clothes, though old and worn, were decent and relatively clean. Not something most workhands cared about in her experience. She thought back to his large hands. Despite their callouses, they were not ingrained with dirt. Unaccountably, she wondered what it would feel like to have them touch her body, then her face flamed at the thought.

Turning onto her back, she wondered at the restless feeling that her imaginings brought on. Her clothes felt too tight, despite the fact that she wasn't wearing stays. Bewilderingly her breasts tingled, and she felt a strange throb in between her legs. Was this what Tempy meant when she used to wax lyrically about her husband Adam? Naturally, both Charity and Chastity were not supposed to be privy to such private conversations between their older sisters, but neither twin had ever paid much attention to such strictures, and eavesdropping had always been only one of their many dubious talents.

Sighing, Charity determinedly shut her eyes. She was being entirely foolish, mooning over a man she'd just met and knew nothing about. That was the kind of thing Chastity did, not her. She was the practical twin. The one that called a spade a spade and had no qualms about offering her opinion, whether wanted or no.

In truth, Charity was certain that should Jago Cardell ever get to know her, he wouldn't actually like her very much.

CHARITY

∞∞∞

Jago was late finishing his shift, which gave him the perfect reason to excuse himself from joining the Shacklefords for dinner. But for some unholy reason, he didn't cry off, and neither did he question his haste in washing himself down back at his lodgings. A pair of forthright brown eyes and softly curling chestnut hair felt as though they were indelibly engraved on his brain. Why Charity Shackleford should have such an effect on him, he had no idea. His head wasn't usually turned so easily.

He'd known his fair share of women, though admittedly most of them had been light skirts sought out on rare visits to Truro. In truth, before his sister's death, Jago had seldom left Tredennick and the tin mine that had provided his family with their wealth for so many years.

While the mine itself was run by Richard Tregear, his father's manager, Jago had always been involved, ever since he was old enough to dip the mineworkers' hats in resin to make them hard. Richard had taught Jago everything he knew.

Morgan Carlyon had never had any interest in the running of the mine, but Jago had lived and breathed it since he was a lad, and his life would be forever linked to the lives of the people who worked there.

Jago squeezed his eyes shut, the longing to be back in Tredennick an almost physical pain. Although he'd revealed his reason for leaving to Richard before he'd left, and had gone with the manager's blessing, Jago feared the mining families he'd abandoned would not be so forgiving when he finally returned home.

Shoving his arms into a clean shirt, Jago forced his thoughts back to the present. Thinking about Wheal Tredennick did no good at all. The sooner he saw Jack swing, the sooner he would be able to return home.

Shrugging on his coat, he ignored the small voice saying if that was the case, why the devil was he wasting his time with a chit clearly only just out of the school room.

∞∞∞

As eight p.m. approached, Charity smoothed down her best gown attempting to get at least some of the creases out. A cast off from … well, one of her older sisters, the dress was plain, without the acres of frothy lace that seemed attached to nearly all of the evening dresses favoured by her older, married siblings. The colour was pleasing, however. A soft apricot which Charity felt emphasised her eyes and made them look less cow like. While she usually managed to disregard Anthony's regular taunts of *Daisy*, she couldn't deny that deep inside, his insults struck a nerve. To Charity's annoyance, her twin's eyes were a deep vivid blue.

'Stay here, Freddy,' she murmured, stroking the foxhound's head. 'I'll bring you back something tasty, I promise.' Then she handed the dog a few pieces of dried mutton and tipped a little of the washing water into his bowl in case he got thirsty.

At the sound of her father's knock, she picked up her gloves and blew out the candle. Not wanting Freddy to be left alone in complete darkness, she'd left the curtains open to allow the bedchamber to benefit from the light cast by the lanterns in the courtyard below so the loss of the only candle in the room did not entirely leave her blind as she made her way to the door.

'Come along, girl, we'll be going down for deuced breakfast if you take much longer,' the Reverend grouched from the landing. Ignoring his impatient tones, Charity took the time to pull on her gloves, finishing her ensemble before opening the door. Why it should matter so, she didn't wish to contemplate.

Her father couldn't quite hide his surprise when she finally appeared. He didn't say anything however, though she couldn't prevent the sudden flush of colour rushing to her cheeks at his knowing look.

The dubious light cast by the sconces on the wall distorted the landing and stairs, forcing them both to take their time negotiating the steep uneven steps. 'Where has Percy been placed?' Charity questioned as she descended carefully, all the while gripping the banister and staring determinedly at the floor. A broken leg she was persuaded would not help matters at all.

'He's at the back near John's room,' Reverend Shackleford muttered, entirely focused on putting one foot in front of another. 'Tare an' hounds I'll be breaking me neck on these deuced stairs if we stay here much longer.'

'Be careful, Father,' Charity admonished, her heart in her mouth as she watched him stumble.

It became a little easier as they reached the landing below, and Charity's thoughts inevitably returned to Jago Cardell. 'Do you suppose Mr Cardell may be able to assist us with the problem of Mary?' she questioned, referring to her father's comment in the coffee shop earlier. The Reverend hmphed in response which she took to mean he thought it unlikely.

'I don't believe he is any part of the smuggling ring,' she persisted, 'and in Nicholas's absence, we certainly need *somebody* to advise us in the best course of action.'

'I'm certain the Almighty has a plan,' her father answered with a grimace. 'He just hasn't shared it with me yet.'

Charity gave a frustrated sigh. 'I don't doubt that for one minute, Father. But consider that the Lord's plan might well be the fortuitous appearance of Mr Cardell. And you're always saying that God helps those who help themselves.'

The Reverend hmphed again as they arrived at the entrance to the small dining room. 'And what makes you think Mr Cardell is in any position to help us?' he argued as they were shown to a table in the corner. Charity waited until they were both seated before answering. 'I don't, but we must effect Mary's release by whatever means necessary and to do so, we cannot close our minds to any course of action.' She sighed and picked up her napkin.

'Mayhap if we simply offer a few hints as to the problem during dinner, we can ascertain whether or not he can lend us his aid,' she suggested, just as Percy arrived.

'Yes, well, whatever you do, do *not* mention that your brother-in-law is the Duke of Blackmore. I cannot imagine any good will come of revealing that particular connection, given the circumstances.' Reverend Shackleford paused and looked over towards the empty doorway. 'In truth the man may not be coming at all,' he observed, 'seeing as it's now ten past the hour and there's no sign of him.'

Charity was surprised at the surge of disappointment she felt at the thought that Jago Cardell might not join them. 'I am certain if he found himself unable to attend, he would have informed us of the fact,' she declared, privately wondering if she was trying to convince her father or herself.

Percy was white faced and uncommunicative and initially refused the Reverend's suggestion of a tankard of ale, only capitulating when sternly informed it was his duty to keep his strength up. Charity was just ordering a small glass of wine, when her heart gave a dull thud as their guest suddenly appeared at the entrance to the dining room. 'Would you be so good as to escort the gentleman at the doorway to this table?' she asked of the serving maid, uncomfortably aware of how breathless her voice sounded.

'Remember, you were very happy to consider Mr Cardell as a possible ally just a few short hours ago,' she urged her father as they watched their guest make his way over to their table. 'Ah, Mr Cardell,' she proclaimed, 'how pleasant it is to see you again.' The large man gave a small bow. 'The honour is mine, Miss Shackleford,' he responded. 'Please forgive my tardiness. Unfortunately, my shift finished late.'

'Well you are here now,' Charity smiled, 'and that's all that matters.'

To her relief, although Percy remained quiet, her father made an effort towards lively conversation. It wasn't difficult. Jago Cardell was both eloquent and amusing, furthering Charity's suspicion that he was much more than he seemed. His eyes also strayed to hers on more than one occasion, and her heart soared as she dared to believe he found her at least a little attractive. It wasn't until they'd nearly finished their main course that the question of their presence in Dartmouth was finally raised.

'We are here at the request of Percy's mother,' Reverend Shackleford offered carefully with a nod towards the reticent curate.

'Oh, is the lady ill?' asked Jago.

'No, she's in gaol.'

The silence in response to Percy's abrupt declaration was deafening. 'I'm sorry, I cannot simply sit here and make polite conversation any longer,' the curate continued defensively. 'Either Mr Cardell can help us, or he cannot. And if he is in the pay of this ... Jack person, then I alone must face the consequences. She is after all my mother.'

'What do you know of Jack?' questioned Jago sharply, his face turning hard and closed in complete contrast to his earlier light-heartedness. Charity's stomach roiled unpleasantly at his tone.

Augustus Shackleford cast a quick glare towards Percy, then gave a resigned sigh and told their guest exactly why they were in Dartmouth and what had happened earlier that day. *So much for offering a few hints*, Charity thought a trifle hysterically.

'So your mother is the infamous Mary Noon?' was all Jago said when the Reverend fell silent.

'I was not aware she was considered so,' murmured Percy despondently. 'We do not have a … a close relationship. Especially given my calling.' He gestured towards his cassock.

'I knew her in Salcombe,' Jago continued. 'I was not aware she'd been arrested.' To Charity's relief, his voice had lost its hard edge. 'How is it you think I can help?'

'Are you involved with this … *Jack*, Mr Cardell?' Charity asked abruptly, watching his response carefully.

Jago stared back at her, his expression giving nothing away. When he didn't answer immediately, Charity began to feel sick, thinking they'd made a terrible, terrible mistake. The relief she felt when he finally said, 'No, I am not,' almost made her giddy.

No one spoke as he took a long draft of his ale and signalled to the serving maid to bring him and the other two men a brandy. When the maid had left, taking his empty tankard away, Jago finally turned back to the still silent table and took a deep breath.

'It's my belief that the man was responsible for the cold-blooded murder of my sister.' He paused and swallowed before telling them what had happened. 'I have spent the last two years of my life trying to bring him to justice.' His voice as he finished, which up to then had been carefully emotionless, suddenly broke. 'Two years,' he ground out, his voice ragged with suppressed pain, 'and I still don't even know what the bastard looks like.'

There was another stunned silence, this time from shock. Until Charity spoke up, her voice barely above a whisper.

'I do.'

CHAPTER 9

Jago could not contain his exhilaration at the thought that he'd finally met someone who could identify the Hope Cove gang's leader. He didn't doubt that a select few were aware of Jack's real identity, but none would be prepared to risk the bastard's wrath by leaking it to the authorities.

When Charity Shackleford described the circumstances in which she'd come across the notorious smuggler, his admiration for her increased tenfold. Her father unsurprisingly was not quite as awestruck.

'I cannot believe you were so bacon-brained that you left your chamber in the middle of the night to wander the halls of a … a … public establishment,' he fumed. 'Not to mention nearly being put to bed with a mattock and tucked up with a deuced spade should the madman have spotted you. Just you wait until I inform Nicholas, my girl.'

'I really don't think you wish to go down *that* particular route, Father,' Charity responded tartly.

To Jago's surprise, she didn't seem in the least cowed. He wondered who Nicholas was. 'So you are certain he was not aware you were privy to his conversation with the innkeeper?' he questioned, putting an end to their argument.

'Definitely not.' Charity shuddered. 'As Father so succinctly put it, I truly do not think I would be sitting here now had he known I was there.'

'So, the innkeeper of this establishment is involved,' mused Jago. 'It's no surprise, in truth. He's known to be a slippery character.'

'He was certainly scared,' Charity conceded. 'Whatever hold this Jack has over him, he enforces it with fear.'

'The man is ruthless,' Jago agreed. 'He cares about nothing but profit and does not balk at the use of the most extreme violence against any who cross him.' He took a sip of his brandy. 'That said, his almost legendary viciousness and the number of bodies washing up along this section of coast have brought him to the attention of the wider authorities, forcing the local Customs officers to get off their arses and do something about him.'

'If you manage to find evidence against him, will you report it to the authorities?' Charity asked evenly. 'Or will you take matters into your own hands?'

Jago stared at her. In truth, he'd shied away from thinking about what he would actually do once he discovered the means to end the smuggler's reign of terror. 'It depends on the circumstances,' he hedged.

'Surely, there is no doubt he would swing if he was arrested,' the Reverend declared.

Jago paused before answering. 'The free traders have influential backers,' he said carefully. 'There would most definitely be opposition, and it's a long road to the morning drop.'

'And where does all this leave my mother?' Percy interjected despairingly.

Jago stared over at the white-faced curate, his sympathy visibly apparent. 'It's clear Mary is a pawn in a much bigger game,' he said at length. 'Should she agree to testify against Jack, she is unlikely to reach the witness stand, a fact she's well aware of. She also knows that should Jack fail to have her silenced, she still runs the risk of ending up on the scaffold alongside him.' He finished the rest of his brandy.

'It's nearly midnight. My brain is no longer sharp enough for such a crucial discussion, and I need to sleep. I suggest we meet tomorrow morning at the Fisherman's Rest and continue our conversation then.'

'Nothing will happen to your mother overnight,' he added when Percy looked about to argue. 'It is not in Jack's interest to rock the boat until absolutely necessary.' He looked around the silent table. 'We will come up with a workable plan to free her in the morning,' he finished, his weariness becoming more apparent.

'We are beyond grateful to you, Mr Cardell,' Charity murmured, placing her napkin on the table. Jago shook his head as he moved to slide back her chair. 'It is I who am indebted to you, Miss Shackleford,' he reasoned with a smile. 'For the first time in three years, I'm persuaded I might actually achieve a whole night's sleep.'

∞∞∞

As he began the long walk back to his lodgings, Jago's heart was the lightest it had been since his sister's death. Despite his earlier avowal, his elation was such that he doubted he would get any sleep at all this night.

Tonight's revelations meant he was much closer to putting an end to Jack's murderous activities, and once the bastard received the justice he so richly deserved, Jago would be free at long last to return to

Tredennick. He imagined the conversation he would have with his father. Mayhap the knowledge that Genevieve's murderer had been made to pay for his crimes truly would bring the old man some comfort.

Surprisingly though, the thought of going home didn't bring Jago the same familiar longing, and as he walked, his thoughts kept straying to Charity Shackleford.

He found himself imagining her walking the grounds of Tredennick, standing on the terrace on a beautiful spring day watching the sunlight sparkle on the sea in the distance. Truly, he believed there was no more beautiful place on earth. What would she think of it?

He shook his head to rid it of such fantasies. He knew nothing about her or her family. He knew they hailed from Devon, where the Reverend had a small parish, but almost nothing else.

And anyway, now was not the time for thinking about the future. The most pressing issue was to find the real man behind the guise. They'd have to comb every corner of Dartmouth in the hope Charity would recognise him again. It would be both time-consuming, tedious and above all, dangerous should Jack realise he'd been uncovered.

Sighing, Jago finally arrived at his lodging house. It was an hour past midnight, but though the cold was biting, he feared his room would not be much warmer. Never again would he take for granted the warming pan placed between his bedsheets at home.

Shivering, he searched his breeches for the key. Just as his fingers closed over the bunch hidden in his pocket, a faint noise caught his attention. It had sounded like a stone being dislodged. He paused, sliding his hand slowly out of his pocket, but didn't look round. Seconds later he recognised the sound of a single footstep. Whoever it was, was going to great pains to hide their presence.

Jago tensed and made a pretext of rummaging around in his other pocket as though still looking for his key. Seconds later, he felt the smallest warmth at his back as someone stepped up directly behind him. Without a second thought, Jago spun round, instinctively stepping backwards. He vaguely registered that the man was large and shabbily dressed before all his attention focused on the knife in the ruffian's hand. Then everything seemed to go at a snail's pace. As the stranger lifted the knife, Jago drew back the fist still holding his bunch of keys and without hesitation, threw everything he had into a punch which met the stranger's nose with a satisfying crack.

With a soft groan the man let go of the knife and went down, blood pouring down the front of his face. The keys had turned Jago's fist into an iron club. Swiftly the Cornishman knelt down, his knee pressing down hard against the ruffian's stomach. 'If you think to rob me, you've chosen the wrong victim,' he hissed.

The man tried to speak, but clearly his nose was broken. Dragging him upright, Jago recognised one of the fishermen from the docks, and with an abrupt sense of dread, realised the cull wasn't here to steal from him.

'Jack wants to know wot you know,' the man finally managed. 'An' 'e's run out o' patience.' Unbelievably, the smuggler grinned, the blood showing dark against his teeth. 'An' 'e ain't goin' to take kindly to you ruining me pretty face. You got 'til sunset tomorrow afore you're done.'

Jack had sent him. The leader of the Hope Cove gang had clearly decided he did want the mythical information Jago claimed to have, but unfortunately preferred to kill him rather than recruit him to get it.

The news held him rigid for a second, and the man immediately took advantage of his brief distraction. Thrusting his hips upwards, he bucked Jago off his stomach, scrambled to his feet and ran, droplets of blood trailing behind him.

Jago didn't give chase. Instead he sat down on the cold ground and waited for his heart rate to settle back to something approaching normal. He'd been a bloody fool to think he could play someone as ruthless as the notorious smuggler.

He'd come to Jack's attention alright, but not in the way he'd hoped. Jago had thought there was no urgency to their search. He'd been wrong.

Now he'd succeeded in sending the gang leader's minion packing with a bloody nose, Jack would consider him even more of a problem, and Jago didn't think the bastard would waste any time before sending others to do the job. The question was, would he wait until tomorrow's sunset to do it?

∞∞∞

Reverend Shackleford quietly stuck his head into Charity's bedchamber to collect Freddy just after dawn. As he clipped on the hound's lead, he made sure to offer a murmured thanks to the Almighty that, on this occasion, his daughter remained sleeping. Undoubtedly, she'd have had something to say if she'd discovered where he was going next.

Next, he tiptoed down to Percy's room where he was surprised to find the curate already dressed. 'Tare an' hounds you look as though you're about to hand in your dinner pail,' was his first comment as the small man opened the door.

When there was no response, the Reverend frowned. 'Right then, Percy Noon, it's about time you got a deuced backbone. Indulging in a fit of the blue devils won't help anything at all, and we've got work to do.'

'What kind of work?' asked the curate, frowning.

'Put on your cloak, and follow me lad. I'm not entirely sure whether our Mr Cardell might be cutting a bit of a wheedle, given that he spent most the evening making calf eyes at Charity.'

'He seemed to know what he was talking about,' Percy defended. 'I actually thought him very amenable.'

'I could tell that when you gave him the whole sorry story, chapter and verse,' the Reverend retorted.

'If I remember rightly, that was you, Sir. I simply told him my mother happened to be in gaol. And anyway, he had a very sad account of his own to share. One much worse than ours.'

'That doesn't mean he wasn't shamming it. The story he gave us could have been a deuced Canterbury tale as far as we know.'

'So how do you intend to find out if he was telling the truth?'

'Last night he claimed to know Mary. I think we should pay an early morning visit to your mother and ask her if that's true.'

'I'm not sure my mother will want to speak with us,' fretted Percy as he followed the Reverend towards the inn's front door.

'Well, Cardell reckons he can get her to safety, I'd have thought that was a good enough reason for her to tell us everything she knows about him. Especially if he's pitching the gammon.'

'You don't know my mother,' Percy grimaced, lifting his cassock out of the filth as they stepped out of the inn. 'If a more contrary woman has ever lived, then I certainly haven't met her.'

'Since when have you become such an expert on women's behaviour,' the Reverend snorted.

As they crossed over into Hanover Place, Augustus Shackleford's determined march faltered. Frowning, he looked around. Though early, he'd have expected a guard to be posted outside the gaol, but there looked to be no one. Continuing towards the front entrance at a slower pace, he finally noticed that the large door was ajar.

'Thunder an' turf,' he muttered, picking up his pace again. Seconds later, they pushed open the door and entered the gaol. This time there were no candles, and the room was almost pitch black.

It was also empty.

CHAPTER 10

Slowly, Charity became aware that the pounding she'd thought in her head was in actual fact someone knocking on the door. She sat up, wincing and holding her head as she did so. The two glasses of wine she'd indulged in last night were clearly taking their toll.

'Charity, are you in there?' Her father's voice was even louder than usual. Without immediately answering, Charity looked round. The light shone through the gap in the curtains, enough to show her that her furry bed companion was missing. 'Have you got Freddy?' was her eventual response.

'Who else would give the deuced cur houseroom,' her father responded, irritation evident in his voice. 'Can I come in?'

'Well, clearly you already have once this morning,' Charity answered clambering out of bed and putting on her robe.

'Is that a yes?' yelled the Reverend, just as she threw open the door.

'Yes,' she snapped into his startled face. 'Seriously, Father,' she continued, walking over to the window, 'do you make a habit of entering many women's bedchambers without so much as a by your leave? I'm persuaded if that is the case, my stepmother will almost certainly have something to say about it.'

The Reverend blanched. 'I simply came to take Freddy to do his business,' he defended. 'And I only stuck my head through the door. Judging by your snoring, you wouldn't have noticed if the King of England had walked in.'

'So did he?' she continued pulling open the curtains.

'Did he what?'

'Did Freddy do his business?' she answered, struggling to contain her exasperation.

The Reverend looked down at the foxhound with a frown. Freddy wagged his tail hopefully. 'I've no deuced idea,' he answered at length, 'and anyway, it doesn't matter. The gaol was empty.'

'Why on earth did you take Freddy to the gaol to do his business?' Charity demanded.

'What? I didn't ta... Oh for ... *balderdash*. Are you listening, Charity? *The gaol was empty.*'

Charity blinked at her father's use of an unfamiliar epithet, then his words finally sank in.

Mary was gone.

'Do you think she escaped or was taken?'

The Reverend shook his head. 'There was no sign of any force, and the rushes on the floor didn't look as if anyone had been dragged over them. I think she must have walked out. Whether she did so willingly, there's no way to tell...' He paused, then added, 'Except there was no guard.'

'Botheration,' exclaimed Charity. 'So Mary could simply have been freed, or the guard could have been in league with the smugglers and allowed them to take her. Where's Percy?'

'He's on his way to the Customs office.'

Charity grimaced. 'I think you should go after him, Father, while I get dressed. It will do no good to antagonise the Customs officer, and while Percy is undeniably eloquent in the pulpit, I'm uncertain he has the necessary diplomacy when dealing with the authorities. The last thing we need is Percy replacing his mother in her cell.' She paused, then added, 'Leave Freddy with me.'

To his own surprise, Reverend Shackleford simply nodded without taking umbrage at his daughter's high-handedness. Charity might well be outspoken, not to mention downright annoying most of the time, but things could have been infinitely worse. He could have been landed with Chastity.

'I will meet you and Percy at the Fisherman's Rest as we planned,' she called after him. 'We'll seek Mr Cardell's advice when we have more information.'

Reverend Shackleford confined his answer to a wave before shutting the door. He didn't think now was the time to tell her his distrust of Jago Cardell was the reason he'd been at the gaol in the first place

∞∞∞

It took the Reverend a mere ten minutes to catch up with Percy. Mainly because his curate didn't know where the Customs office was located and had spent the last half an hour marching up and down the harbour. With his cassock flapping behind him, he resembled a large black crow.

'Tare an' hounds, Percy,' the Reverend admonished when he finally caught up with him. 'What the deuce is wrong with you, lad? You've got a tongue in your head, haven't you?'

'This whole smoky business has me at sixes and sevens,' Percy blurted. 'I can't seem to think straight, Sir.'

Strangely, Reverend Shackleford's irritation was overtaken by an unaccustomed sympathy towards his hapless curate, so he refrained from remarking that thinking straight had never been one of Percy's strengths. Instead, he patted the smaller man's arm and went to ask for directions.

It turned out the Customs House was located on Bayard's Cove, a mere stone's throw from where they were standing. 'Right then, Percy, make sure to let me do the talking,' ordered the Reverend as he led the way. Percy nodded his head vigorously, for once in complete accord with his superior.

Situated only yards away from where the Mayflower had set sail nearly two hundred years earlier, the office of His Majesty's Customs and Excise was a handsome building of two stories set on the cobbled quayside of Bayard's Cove at the southern end of the harbour. The wharf was protected at the very end by a small artillery fort, which looked to be no longer in use. The boats docked here were considerably smaller than the two merchant vessels they'd seen earlier and comprised mostly fishing boats.

It would have been a picturesque spot if not for the stench of fish and the cacophony of voices belonging to the numerous fishermen mending nets. Clearly, their catch had already been offloaded and moved.

The door to the Customs House sat open, and outside, two men were arguing heatedly. Without pause Reverend Shackleford stepped towards them, intending to enquire whether the Customs officer might be found within. Before he'd taken a step however, Percy gripped the clergyman's arm urgently. 'It's him,' he muttered nodding his head towards the two men still in a heated discussion. 'Joseph Smith. The *prison guard*,' he added when the Reverend looked at him blankly.

'Which one is he? I haven't got my eyeglasses with me.' The Reverend squinted towards the two men as Percy whispered, 'The one on the left.'

'Are you certain?' Augustus Shackleford frowned as the guard suddenly threw his hands in the air and stomped away, heading back towards the centre of the town. 'Quick,' the Reverend hissed, grabbing hold of Percy's arm in turn and dragging the curate in pursuit.

'What are we doing?' Percy questioned as he hurried to keep up with his superior. 'I thought we were going to speak to the Customs officer.'

'This Joseph Smith might well be involved in your mother's kidnapping,' Reverend Shackleford retorted without slowing his pace. 'He could have her stashed somewhere.'

'Aren't you being a little hasty, Sir? We don't even know that she's been kidnapped,' protested Percy. 'She could be on her way to Salcombe as we speak.'

The Reverend snorted. 'And she might be floating there with a deuced boulder attached to her big toe if she put a rub in the way of the smugglers' plans,' he answered bluntly. As he finished speaking, their quarry turned left and started up a set of steep stairs set in between two narrow houses. Hesitating at the bottom, the clergyman stuck his head round the corner just in time to see Joseph Smith disappear through a door almost at the top.

'What should we do now, Sir?' whispered Percy.

Augustus Shackleford frowned. 'Mayhap there's a back way in?' he ventured, starting up the stairs.

By the time they reached the top, the Reverend was convinced he was about to have an apoplexy. It was only the thought of having to greet the Almighty wearing his second-best cassock that prevented him toppling backwards. That, and Percy pushing him up the steps from behind.

'Right then, Percy lad,' he wheezed when they finally reached the top step, 'just give me a couple of minutes, and I'll be good as new.'

The curate eyed his red-faced sweating superior doubtfully. 'Are you certain you should be doing this, Sir?' he questioned.

'I can't lie, Percy,' the Reverend puffed in response. 'This fearless leader business is not all it's cracked up to be.' He closed his eyes and shook his head, the action causing him to wobble ominously close to the top of the steps. 'But if not me, who?' he implored sadly, shaking his head again and wobbling back the other way.

Percy watched the swaying with his heart in his mouth, murmuring a silent prayer when the Reverend finally sat down on the top step.

Satisfied that his superior was not suddenly about to meet his maker from the bottom of a fifty-foot flight of stairs, Percy turned his attention to their surroundings. Looming behind them, two tired looking cottages were squeezed together facing down towards the street below, effectively cutting out much of the natural light even though it was still early in the day. Percy could see no candlelight, nor any sign of movement and wondered if perhaps they were used for storage.

He turned his attention to the house they'd seen Joseph Smith disappear into nearly ten minutes ago now. Initially he didn't think there was any space behind it but on looking more carefully, he saw that what he thought was a dead end, was in actual fact a narrow passageway. He'd nearly missed it due to a large barrel blocking the entrance. 'Sir,' he breathed, 'I think there might be a way in.'

The Reverend peered into the blackness in the direction of the curate's pointing finger. 'Tare an' hounds, I think you're right,' he muttered, clambering to his feet and hurrying over to the barrel. Giving it an experimental shove, he realised it was empty. 'Give me a hand Percy,' he said excitedly. Together they heaved the barrel out of the way and stared into the darkness.

The Reverend took a hesitant step forward, peering into the gloom. The ground was soft underfoot from the accumulation of debris. 'I can't see a door,' he whispered back to Percy who was practically sitting on his shoulders.

'I'm not sure this is a good idea, Sir,' the curate muttered. 'I mean it's so dark in here, we could be treading in ... well, *anything*.' He lifted his foot out of the muck, and bent his head, sniffing experimentally.

'Don't be so chuckleheaded, Percy,' Reverend Shackleford whispered back, nonetheless lifting his cassock. 'Faint heart never won fair lady,' he intoned, then paused before adding, 'Though I don't think old Francis Drake had your mother in mind when he spoke the words.'

He gave a soft chuckle and took another cautious step forward. Seconds later, they could see the end of the passageway. Augustus Shackleford sighed, thinking they were out of luck, until he took one more step, and his foot made a different sound. 'There's wood under here,' he hissed excitedly to Percy. 'Help me shift this muck.'

Cringing, Percy helped the Reverend kick aside the sludge underfoot. 'I think that was a rat,' he shuddered as something landed against the wall with a soft plop.

Seconds later, they'd revealed a trap door set into the ground. 'Where do you suppose it leads?' Percy asked fearfully.

'There's only one way to find out.' Reverend Shackleford bent down and took hold of a small ring set into the wood. 'I hope that's not rat innards,' he muttered, shaking something squidgy off his finger. Percy made a retching sound but didn't answer.

'Right then, here goes.' Taking a deep breath, the Reverend heaved, expecting the door to be sealed shut. To his surprise the wood lifted immediately, and momentum had him toppling backwards, landing on his arse with a low whoomph.

'Fiend seize it,' he muttered, struggling to his feet and attempting to see if anything nasty was sticking to his nether regions.

'I think it might be a cellar,' mused Percy, ignoring his superior's capers and peering into the blackness.

'Can you see how far the floor is,' the Reverend questioned, finally abandoning his efforts to inspect his backside.

'It's too dark to see,' the curate whispered back.

The Reverend bent down next to him, and Percy wrinkled his nose. 'Right then, I'll have to lower you down,' the large man muttered.

'What?' Percy squeaked. 'But we don't know what's down there?'

'And we're not likely to find out unless we have a look,' retorted the Reverend matter-of-factly. 'And at least you're not going to have to lie in deuced rat droppings.'

'Would it not be better to go a fetch Mr Cardell?' Percy stalled. 'I mean, he's quite … well … *large*. He could probably jump down.'

'Have you lost what little wit you have, Percy Noon?' the Reverend exclaimed. 'We don't know which side Cardell is on. We could end up locked in with your mother.'

'We don't even know she's down there,' repeated Percy, his voice turning desperate.

'She's down there alright,' Augustus Shackleford replied with far more conviction than he was feeling. But they'd come this far. 'Come on, Percy lad, get a deuced backbone. I promise I won't let you go…'

CHAPTER 11

Reasoning it would take her father some time to find his curate and speak with the Custom's officer, Charity took time over her toilette. She'd only brought two day dresses with her, and neither was particularly flattering. Still, there was nothing she could do about that, and anyway she would be unlikely to remove her pelisse when they met Mr Cardell…

Her musings came to a screeching halt.

This was the first time in her nearly nineteen years that she'd actually cared what a gentleman thought of her. What was it about Mr Cardell that made him different to all the other gentlemen she'd met?

She frowned, seating herself at the small dressing table. To be fair, she hadn't exactly met an overabundance of gentlemen. In fact, the only ones she'd had any dealings with at all had been her sisters' husbands. She was not given to lively chatter like Chastity, and up until recently, any large gathering had been an excuse to kick up a lark.

She picked up a brush and drew it through her hair thoughtfully, trying to examine her feelings for Jago Cardell. What did she know about him really? Oh he was handsome as sin with his honey-coloured eyes and wheat-ripened hair. He'd told them that his home was in Cornwall and that his sister had been cruelly murdered nearly three years earlier. But that was it.

Thinking back, she realised just how careful he'd been when divulging information about himself. But then, she and her father had been just as reticent. Revealing nothing about their connection to the Duke of Blackmore or indeed exactly where they called home, aside from it being in Devon.

How on earth could any kind of a relationship develop between them when they couldn't even admit to each other where they lived? And did she actually *want* something more with the enigmatic Cornishman?

Three short days ago she could not have dreamed she'd be having thoughts such as these. She'd been resigned to simply helping her sister make a good marriage. Her heart had never beat faster in a man's presence, and she'd never even contemplated the thought of man's lips against hers … and more.

Behind her Freddy gave a loud snore, breaking her reverie. With a sigh, she abandoned her daydreaming. Whatever her feelings for Jago Cardell, now was not the time to act upon them. She knew he found her attractive, but she was worldly enough to realise that that on its own meant very little to a man. She must put her fantasising aside and concentrate on the task at hand.

She looked down at her watch chain. Goodness, she had only half an hour before their meeting in the coffee house. She sincerely hoped her father had succeeded in speaking with the Customs officer and that Mary Noon had merely been released rather than kidnapped as they'd feared.

Swiftly pinning her hair up, she donned her pelisse, threw on her cloak and finally tugged on her boots. In less than ten minutes, she and Freddy were out of the inn's front door and making their way along the Quay towards the Fisherman's Rest. Turning the corner, she spied a small butcher's shop on the opposite side of the street. Mayhap Freddy would enjoy a nice, tasty bone for his dinner this night instead of scraps from their table, and she still had plenty of time before the coming rendezvous. Lifting her skirts, she hastened towards the other side of the street and joined the small queue waiting to be served.

As she moved up the line, she quickly tied Freddy up outside before entering the shadowy interior of the shop, wrinkling her nose at the coppery smell. Her attention on the large cuts of meat hanging on the walls, she wasn't immediately aware it was her turn. With a quick apologetic glance at the people still behind her, she turned towards the butcher, intending to ask if they had any leftover mutton bones, but the words died in her throat when she looked up. Straight into the eyes of the elusive Jack.

∞∞∞

'You won't let me go will you, Sir?' Percy implored in a heated whisper as he sat down on the edge of the opening.

'Stop being so deuced lily livered,' Reverend Shackleford retorted. 'Have I ever dropped you before?'

'Yes,' Percy came back bluntly.

The Reverend opened his mouth to deny such a monstrous accusation, but abruptly remembering the *one or two* occasions when he *may* have been less than solicitous of his curate's person, he shut it again.

'If we're going to rescue Mary, *one* of us has to go down there,' he reasoned instead. 'And you know I'd be the one risking life and limb if I could, Percy. I mean, how often do the villagers at Blackmore declare *daring* my middle name.'

'I thought it was Edward,' Percy answered with a frown.

Reverend Shackleford stared nonplussed at his curate for a full second before shaking his head and muttering, 'Sometimes, Percy

Noon, I think you've got nothing but deuced fresh air between your ears.'

Then with a long-suffering sigh, he got down onto his hands and knees and instructed Percy to turn round until they were facing each other. 'Right then,' the Reverend went on. 'I'll hold onto your hands while you … well … you know … while you just …'

'Just what?' Percy blurted. Sensing the small man was about to bolt, the Reverend grabbed hold of his trembling hands and gave an encouraging push.

With a strangled squeak, Percy obligingly slid backwards until only his upper torso was above the lip of the hole.

Panic stricken, the curate let go of one of the Reverend's hands and made a grab for the large man's shoulder. Unfortunately, his questing hand entirely missed its intended mark and instead planted his superior a prime facer that had the Reverend seeing stars. With a muffled grunt, Augustus Shackleford toppled forward with Percy clinging on to his head like a limpet.

Then, slowly but surely both men slid into the hole.

∞∞∞

It was him. Charity was entirely certain. Her heart hammered against her chest, and she fought the urge to turn tail and run. He stood silently, waiting to hear what she wanted and for a few seconds she struggled to remember what she'd come in for. Fortunately, at that moment, a jovial voice yelled from outside the shop. 'You got any sweetbreads in there, George? I ain't standing 'ere freezing me ballocks off if they're all gone.'

Jack took his eyes off Charity and glanced towards the speaker. 'All gone, Paddy,' he answered. 'Best try again tomorrow.' His voice was so different from the sinister, threatening tone she'd heard him use in the inn, that for a second she thought she'd been mistaken, until his eyes returned to hers, watchful, guarded. 'I haven't got all day, miss,' he commented mildly.

Swallowing, Charity asked if he had any mutton bones. She wondered if he could hear the wobble in her voice, and the urge to dash out of the shop was almost overwhelming.

'Reckon I might have a couple out the back,' he answered. 'They for the dog?' He tipped his head towards Freddy, currently drooling through the window.

Charity nodded. As he disappeared behind an old, tattered curtain, she silently berated herself for her cowardice. Her behaviour was that of a chit still in the school room. Certainly not that of a woman walking out on her own. She took a few deep breaths, and by the time he returned a couple of minutes later, she'd managed to get her heart rate under control.

'Not much meat on them,' he observed, holding the two bones up for her inspection, 'but plenty of good marrow.' She coolly nodded her acceptance and busied herself opening her purse as she waited for him to wrap them up in some old newspaper.

'That'll be three pennies.'

Handing over the coin, she thanked him courteously, and even managed a small nod as she took the package and calmly made her way out of the shop. Once outside, her composure began to crumble as she fumbled to untie Freddy as quickly as possible. Indeed, she was so focused on her task that she did not see the smugglers' leader step round the counter to stare after her thoughtfully.

Walking swiftly, she arrived at the Fisherman's Rest earlier than the allotted time, but after hesitating on the threshold for a few moments, she finally decided that as a woman grown she would be foolish to remain outside in the cold and risk an ague or worse when she would be perfectly cosy inside.

Indeed, as she pushed open the door, she determined she would go one step further and treat herself to a hot chocolate while she waited for the three men to arrive.

∞∞∞

On waking, Jago had realised he dared not return to work. He had until sunset to supply Jack with some kind of useful information, but somehow, he didn't think he'd got that long. Especially given that he was pulling the wool over the smuggler's eyes. In reality, he had nothing.

Jago had played it all wrong. He'd tried too hard and come to Jack's attention for all the wrong reasons. He'd survived two of the gang leader's ruffians, but he wasn't sure he would manage to outwit a third. And the last two attacks had merely been warnings.

He had to discover Jack's real identity. Today. If he left without knowing who the smuggler really was, he wouldn't get another chance. Once he had that information, he could take it to the authorities and let them deal with the bastard. He forced his mind from the possibility that Jack was likely in the pay of someone much higher up. Someone who might well thwart every effort to see the murderer hang.

Jago had finally acknowledged that he couldn't do the deed himself. Vengeance had kept him on this path since Genevieve's death. He hadn't cared what happened to him if he was caught and convicted for putting an end to Jack's reign of terror. But that had changed since his chance meeting with Charity Shackleford. After so long, he finally dared to hope that he had something to live for.

But now was not the time to be thinking about happy ever afters. They had to survive the day first. Climbing out of bed, he splashed his face with cold water and threw on his clothes, his nose wrinkling at their slightly musty odour. It had been so long since he'd given any consideration to how he looked or indeed smelled. To the people he'd mixed with for the last two years, washing was something that happened if you fell into the sea.

He left everything but the clothes he was wearing. He wouldn't be coming back. He laid the keys along with the coin for his rent on top of the small cot and slipped out of the door.

As he began the long walk back to town, he concentrated on what he needed to do. Identify Jack, find a way to free the curate's disreputable mother and get all of them to a place of safety. But even if Charity was unable to identify Jack, Jago had to leave Dartmouth before dusk, and he could not leave Charity and her father behind.

Their connection to Mary Noon, and more tenuously to him, would eventually bring them to Jack's attention. And as Jago had learned to his cost, the smuggler did not allow any loose ends.

∞∞∞

'Sir, Sir ... *Sir*,' Percy's frantic whispers finally penetrated the fog, and Augustus Shackleford opened his eyes. 'Oh, thank God,' the curate responded fervently.

Blinking, the Reverend stared up into the grimy face only inches away from his. The meagre light cast from the open trap door above gave the curate an almost demonic appearance, and for one horrified second, the Reverend thought he'd cocked up his toes and ended up downstairs.

'Thunder an' turf,' he muttered when Percy finally came into focus. 'What the deuce happened?'

'We fell,' Percy answered gruffly, hoping his superior might have forgotten the bit that came before it. The Reverend struggled into a sitting position and looked round. Fortunately, they'd fallen on an empty pile of sacks. Though bruised and battered, neither man appeared to have broken anything. 'How long have we been here?'

'A few minutes, I think.'

Climbing unsteadily to his feet, Reverend Shackleford waited for his eyes to adjust to the gloom. Gradually, he began to make out barrels and boxes, all stacked on top of one another. 'God help us, Percy,' he breathed. 'This is where they stash the deuced contraband.'

'What are we going to do, Sir?' Percy's voice wavered as he fought to control his panic.

'Well, we can't go back the way we came in,' the Reverend retorted, 'so we just have to hope that once we've found Mary, there'll be another way out.'

'Do you really think she's here, Sir?'

Reverend Shackleford nodded. 'She's here, lad. If that Joseph Smith isn't a deuced ivory turner, I'll eat your next sermon.' He looked round, 'Right then, there's got to be a door. That hole up there can't be the only way in. The tub men would likely have an apoplexy if they had to carry the barrels up those steps.'

A minute or so later, sure enough, they spotted a low door in the far corner. 'Stay behind me,' Reverend Shackleford ordered. Unsurprisingly, the curate didn't argue.

Fortunately, the door was unlocked, and after cautiously easing it open slightly, the Reverend peered through the crack. There was a tallow candle stuck in a crude sconce high on the wall. 'Well, someone's here,' he muttered. 'I can't imagine they'd risk leaving a candle burning otherwise.' He pulled the door wider and stepped out into the narrow corridor, Percy almost attached to him from behind.

The two men tiptoed down the corridor towards a door at the end, just in time to hear the less than dulcet tones of Percy's mother declare that if the bloody jackanape came any closer, she'd cut off his baubles and turn 'em into a pair of earrings.

CHAPTER 12

Charity had nearly finished her hot chocolate and was beginning to get a little anxious. It was one thing to decide she was a woman of the world and enter a coffee shop alone for a mere half an hour. It was quite another to remain seated for long enough to become a focus of interest. And she suspected that having a large dog at her feet simply added to the curiosity.

She'd just decided that she would go and look for her father and Percy, when she heard the door open. Looking up hopefully, her heart thudded as she observed Jago Cardell enter the cafe. His stature was such that he seemed to dwarf everyone present. Swallowing, she gave him an uncertain smile. By rights, she should no more be sitting in a coffee house with an unmarried gentleman than she should be sitting on her own. It had not occurred to her that he might arrive before her father, thus leaving her unchaperoned.

Although Mr Cardell did not seem particularly perturbed to find her seated alone, and, smiling back at her, strode over to the table without hesitation. 'May I sit, Miss Shackleford?' he asked for politeness' sake. Charity inclined her head as graciously as her heightened colour would allow. Truly, anyone observing her now would think her a light-skirt.

As Jago Cardell seated himself, the serving maid hurried over to take his order, her side glance of admiration unmistakeable. Unaccountably, Charity found herself irritated at the woman's brazen smile, and as a result, her request for a pot of tea came out more like an order – which of course vexed her all the more. Not that the infuriating wench seemed aware of the glares Charity was casting in her direction, and after favouring the handsome Cornishman with one last coquettish glance, she flounced off into the kitchen with their order.

'Are your father and Percy delayed?' he asked, bending down to give Freddy a fuss.

'I'm certain they will be here presently,' she responded, her tone terse enough to have him look over at her in surprise.

Damn and blast, she thought, berating herself silently. Now was hardly the time for jealousy to rear its ugly head. There was too much at stake. 'Forgive my rudeness, Mr Cardell,' she said contritely. 'I believe I am allowing my anxiety to get the better of me.' Not entirely a lie.

His hurried assurance that she hadn't been rude at all came at the same time as their tea, and this time, Charity was able to offer the shameless chit a gracious smile which she was persuaded would have impressed even Grace. As soon as they were alone again, she took a deep breath. 'I have much to tell you,' she murmured, taking care to keep her voice low. 'I had thought to delay until my father arrived, but I feel the information cannot wait any longer.'

Jago Cardell raised his eyebrows at her statement but did not reply immediately. Indeed, he seemed to be involved in some kind of internal debate, and so she remained silent, unsure whether he wanted her to continue. She was surprised at the tone of his voice when he finally spoke. He seemed almost resigned, but to what she could not tell.

'I too have ... developments to share with you, Miss Shackleford which I believe will affect the discussion we had last night.' He took a sip of his tea, staring at her intently, and she realised he was waiting for her to go first.

Gripping her tea dish with both hands, Charity took another deep breath. 'I've seen Jack,' she whispered. As he stared at her in confusion, she added, 'Today.' She paused and gave a triumphant smile. 'I know who he is.'

She saw the moment her declaration sank in. She'd expected his expression to be triumphant, but instead, all she saw was relief. 'I think his real name is George,' she continued when he didn't speak, 'and he works in the butcher's shop near to the quay.'

'How?' Jago finally managed, wishing the dish he was cradling contained something much, much stronger.

'I think I need to start at the beginning,' Charity said with a sigh, 'which will help shed some light why my father and Percy have been delayed.' She went on to describe exactly what had happened from the moment her father had discovered Mary Noon missing, to her discovery of the elusive Jack's identity.

'Unfortunately, I have no idea where my father and Percy are now,' she finished, unable to keep the concern out of her voice. 'The last we spoke, they were going to discuss Mary's disappearance with the Custom's officer.' She paused before adding ruefully, 'I'd like to say that my father disappearing for several hours at a time is unusual, but in truth, it's not. It drives my stepmother to distraction.'

'Do you think it possible the Reverend has discovered where Mary is and taken matters into his own hands?' Jago asked tightly.

Charity thought for a second. 'His meddling has got him and poor old Percy into more hobbles than I care to remember,' she sighed, 'though I cannot imagine even he would be foolish enough to risk the wrath of a gang of murderous smugglers.'

A sudden commotion coming from the small kitchen drew their attention. 'Ere, wot the devil d'yer think yer doin'?'

Unbelievably, Charity heard her father's voice respond, with the same fervour he usually reserved for reading the final paragraph of one of Percy's epic three-hour sermons.

'You may have been *told* that God works in mysterious ways, my good woman, but you see before you living proof. A sinner who has just this very moment received a message from *On High*. An epiphany you might say.'

'A wot?'

'Indeed, you may actually be the first to witness with your very own eyes my companion's road to Damascus.' The Reverend suddenly appeared in the doorway, looking wildly around. On spotting Charity, his relief was palpable. She had time to wonder why he wasn't wearing his cassock when he suddenly turned back, yelling, 'Praise the Lord,' before yanking a bony individual wearing the missing cassock out of the kitchen.

For a second, Charity stared in confusion at the dirty, wild-haired creature wearing her father's second-best robe. Then, with a thrill of disbelief, she realised the person was none other than Mary Noon. 'Bless you, my son,' she chortled as the Reverend determinedly dragged her towards the door, Percy trailing behind. As he passed their table, he mouthed, 'Percy's room' without stopping. Seconds later, they were gone.

Charity turned back to Jago Cardell who was watching the whole proceedings in disbelief. 'Well, I think we can safely answer your last question,' was all she commented tartly.

∞∞∞

'So how did you get her past Joseph Smith?' Charity asked.

'Well, he's undoubtedly going to have a bit of a headache, but the Almighty must have approved, seeing as he left the mallet there in the first place.' The Reverend shrugged. 'Then we just followed our noses. To be honest I'm not sure I'd be very keen to use that establishment again after seeing inside their deuced kitchen.' He shuddered.

'I assume you didn't kill the guard,' commented Jago drily.

'Certainly not,' Reverend Shackleford retorted, 'but I'm hoping he might be in the land of nod for a good while.'

'Did he see you?' The clergyman shook his head.

The Cornishman sighed and wondered how the devil he'd come to be discussing hitting prison guards over the head with a country vicar. Meanwhile, the curate's mother looked as though she was ready to flee at the first opportunity. 'Were you harmed at all, Mrs Noon?' he asked.

Still wearing the Reverend's cassock, Mary looked as though the last few hours had taken their toll. Underneath the grime, her face was pale and sunken. 'The bastards din't dare knock me around too much, else their lord and master'ed 'ave somethin' to say about it.' She paused and grimaced. 'I just want to go 'ome.'

'Will you be safe there, Mother?' Percy asked, speaking for the first time. The curate too looked as though he was fervently wishing himself elsewhere, and in truth, Jago feared a sudden gust of wind might blow him over.

'You said in the gaol that you wouldn't last five minutes in Salcombe,' the Reverend added doubtfully.

'I've thought about it since. Nobody'll come after me as long as I keep me 'ead down,' Mary Noon retorted. 'Jack only got in a bleeding high dudgeon cos I'd landed meself right under the noses o' the Bluebottles.'

Jago knew she was referring to the Customs officials and asked, 'So what about the Bluebottles, are they likely to drag you back to Dartmouth?'

'I ain't no use to them. They got bigger fish to fry. It woz me own bleeding fault I got caught. Landed in their bloody laps, I did, but they know I won't cry rope on Jack. I might be old, but I ain't dicked in the bleeding nob.'

Jago wondered what the old woman really knew, but looking into her fearful eyes, he realised she'd never divulge any of the smuggler's secrets.

'So, if we leave you in Salcombe, you're certain you'll be safe?' he questioned.

'How are we going to do that?' Charity asked. "I'm not certain our carriage will easily negotiate the roads, such as they are. Not this time of year.'

Jago took a deep breath. 'You can't take her in your carriage any more than you can return home in it,' he declared. 'In fact, you can't return home at all. At least until Jack is arrested.'

'You aiming to bring the bastard down then?' Mary interrupted before anyone else could respond to Jago's shocking announcement.

'Yes,' he answered simply. She stared at him for a second, searching his face, then gave a dark chuckle. 'Good bloody riddance I say. The day that bastard swings, can't come too soon.'

'Why on earth can we not go home?' Charity queried.

'Because he'll find us,' responded the Reverend heavily.

'But he doesn't know who we are or where we live?' she argued.

'The innkeeper does. He knows our names at least. And it would only be a small step for Jack to discover our relationship to Nicholas.'

Nicholas again. It was the second time Jago had heard the name mentioned. Clearly, the man was someone of influence. Mayhap he could help them bring Jack to justice. If they managed to get the bastard arrested in the first place. He made a mental note to probe once they were safely out of Dartmouth.

'And with Nicholas in London and Grace in Torquay,' Reverend Shackleford was saying. 'That leaves only Agnes and the youngens. If we go home, we'll lead these deuced ruffians straight to them.'

'But why on earth would he take time pursuing us?' Charity contended. 'He has no idea what part we have played. And I do not think he…'

She was cut off as Jago, well aware of Mary Noon's interested silence, swiftly interrupted her. 'We can't be sure of anything,' he declared. 'And any measures we take are merely precautionary.' He turned towards Percy's mother. 'Come with me, Mrs. Noon. Let us see to your safety first.' Her eyes narrowed, obviously realising he wanted her gone.

'It's best if you leave now, Mother,' Percy added, placing his hand on her shoulder.

Mary stared at her son and gave a rueful grin. 'Can't wait to be rid of me, 'eh Percy?'

The curate shifted uncomfortably but stood his ground. 'I cannot approve of your actions, Mother,' he murmured, 'but I don't wish any harm to come to you. And if you stay longer in Dartmouth, you may yet end up behind bars again, or worse.'

She sighed and nodded, climbing to her feet. 'Will you come and see me?' she asked, the studied nonchalance in her voice failing to hide her hope.

There was a pause, then Percy nodded. 'I will,' he responded finally.

Satisfied, she gave an answering nod. 'Get a bloody move on then, Cardell,' she sneered, 'I ain't got all day.'

Jago turned to the other three. 'Pack your belongings and tell your carriage driver to be ready. I will be back as soon as I can.'

CHAPTER 13

Charity found her mind replaying the events of the last few days over and over again as she packed her few belongings. The attraction she felt for Jago Cardell paled in the face of the uncertainty she now faced. Where on earth were they going to go? Clearly, wherever the Cornishman had in mind to take them, he did not want Mary Noon to have knowledge of it. She felt sick with fear for her family, and her hands shook so much, she sank down onto the bed and clasped them tightly in her lap to stop their trembling.

Sensing her distress, Freddy whined softly and butted her hand with his head. Stroking him absently, Charity thought back to her scathing comments about her twin's unrestrained behaviour. What if that was the last time she ever saw Chastity? Jago Cardell could even now be making plans to take them to the Americas. A feeling of dread began to well up. She could not, *would not* leave her sister.

She jumped as a loud knock on the door put an abrupt end to her rising panic. Grateful for the distraction, she took a deep breath and climbed to her feet. No doubt it was her father thinking to give her another lecture.

To her shock, the person at the door was the subject of her thoughts. 'I'm aware of the impropriety of my request, Miss Shackleford,' he murmured as she stared at him nonplussed, 'but I wish to speak with you urgently. May I come in?'

Her face pink at the thought of allowing a man other than her father into her room, Charity nevertheless moved wordlessly aside. 'You may rest assured that nobody saw me come in, but nonetheless I will get to the point quickly,' he added when she still didn't speak, though she felt her panic begin to rise again at his next words. 'I have reason to believe that Jack suspects you recognised him,' he stated bluntly.

'Why … how?' Charity stammered. 'I assure you I was most circumspect.'

'I do not doubt it, Miss Shackleford, but this man has lived on his wits for years, and he's not survived without developing instincts far superior to most of us.' He walked to the window and looked down into the courtyard, taking care not to be seen.

'How do you know he suspects?' she questioned, joining him.

'Some individuals have been making enquiries about a young woman with a dog,' he answered grimly. 'It's only a matter of time before their questions lead them here.' Turning back, his eyes fell on her travel bag. 'Are you finished packing?'

She nodded, beginning to feel a little lightheaded. 'What about Mary?' she asked, fighting down her nausea.

'Gone,' Jago replied. 'She has safe passage aboard a fishing boat bound for Salcombe.' He took a deep breath. 'You, your father and Percy must be ready to depart at high tide,' he continued, his voice brooking no argument.

'Where are you taking us?' Charity whispered, her fear overtaking her. Jago opened his mouth to snap, 'What does it matter,' when he suddenly realised that she was truly distraught. Indeed, she appeared very close to swooning. Swallowing an epithet that had no more place in a lady's bedroom than he did, Jago took a deep breath. Clearly, he was handling this all wrong. All he'd succeeded in doing was frightening her half to death.

'I'm taking you to my home in Cornwall,' he said, deciding that honesty was the best policy. Indeed at this late stage, there was no time for anything else.

'Oh.' His answer seemed to take the wind out of her sails, and he couldn't help but wonder where on earth she thought he was taking them.

'Jack does not know of its existence,' he continued. 'You can stay in safety until the danger to you and your family has passed.'

'But what's to stop Jack sending his hired thugs to Blackmore anyway?' countered Charity.

'Blackmore. Is that where you live?' asked Jago wondering where he'd heard the name before. Charity bit her lip and nodded.

'Jack won't wish to draw attention to himself or his activities unless it's absolutely necessary,' Jago reassured her. 'I'll advise your father to let it slip to the innkeeper that you are going on to Plymouth, and will be there for a sennight,' He paused, thinking quickly. 'It's important you are seen leaving Dartmouth in your carriage, but once at the village of Stoke Fleming, I'll be waiting for you. Your carriage will then continue to Blackmore without you.'

'Will that work?' Charity worried.

'It's the best we can do in the circumstances,' he answered simply. She nodded, grateful he hadn't tried to sugar coat the situation. 'Please be ready to leave within the hour,' he finished, turning towards the door. However, as his hand touched the knob, he stopped and seconds later, turned back towards her, his face grim.

'I've not been entirely honest with you, Miss Shackleford,' he declared roughly. Her pulse quickened at his words, but she said nothing, and after a second, he sighed and continued. 'You are not the only one for whom Jack has murderous designs.'

'You,' Charity confirmed in a whisper, staring into his starkly handsome countenance.

'Me,' he verified drily. She raised her eyebrows and waited for him to continue. 'You're aware I've spent the last two years trying to infiltrate the Hope Cove gang, in the hope of discovering Jack's real identity?' He waited for her answering nod before continuing. 'Well, it seems my efforts to come to his attention succeeded, but not in the way I'd hoped.' He finally shook his head ruefully. 'Unfortunately, it appears I overestimated my spying talents.'

'So what do you do when you're not trying to infiltrate dangerous smuggling rings?' Charity murmured.

'My family owns a tin mine,' he clarified. 'The name Cardell is false. My real name is Jago Carlyon.'

'Does Jack know this?' she questioned. He shook his head in response. 'Then clearly you are not entirely without talent,' she responded with a slight smile.

Unable to help himself, he grinned back at her, his heart unaccountably light in the knowledge that she hadn't condemned him for not revealing the full truth.

'BUT YOU MUST REALISE that by aligning yourselves with me, you could well be sailing into even stormier waters,' he still felt compelled to say.

'There is no one else,' she responded with a shrug. And it was true. In Nicholas's absence, she dared not let her father take charge. She loved him dearly, but his propensity for creating mayhem… Well, spymaster or not, Jago *Carlyon* was their best option.

She tried to ignore the small voice inside her insisting that she could not bear to say goodbye. Not yet. Mayhap, not ever.

'I must go,' he murmured at length, though he'd never wanted anything less. Here it felt as if they were isolated, a step apart from the world. He wondered what it would be like to get to know her. To simply dance, flirt and indulge in witty banter. As soon as the thought arose, he almost laughed out loud. His witty banter was as good as his spying.

'Do you find something amusing, Mr Carlyon?' Charity asked, noticing the sudden quirk in his lips.

Jago threw caution to the winds. 'Only that you must know of my attraction to you, Miss Shackleford, and I was wondering how it would have been if we'd met in a ballroom.'

'And you find that droll?' she quizzed, her heart beating frantically in her chest.

He shook his head and stepped nearer to her. Charity held her ground, staring into golden eyes that made no attempt to conceal the depth of his attraction. 'I was imagining us in conversation,' he murmured wryly. 'And you must know I am not an articulate man.'

'I think anyone who uses the word articulate is one by default,' she whispered, feeling compelled to lessen the sudden *connection* between them.

As if in a dream, she watched him raise his hand and lift the solitary strand of hair away from her face, tucking it behind her ear 'So beautiful,' he murmured, his voice hoarse.

Charity made no move, simply marvelled at the longing in his gaze. Her eyes travelled down to his generous lips, and she felt a sudden throb, deep in her core, as she wondered how it would feel to have him kiss her. His sudden indrawn breath told her he was well aware of the direction of her thoughts. His face almost harsh with effort, he made to step backwards. Without thinking, Charity reached out and touched his chest. 'Please,' she whispered.

With a low groan, Jago stepped forward and pulled her to him, his hands like brands on her shoulders. For a long second, he stared down at her, his torment clear. Then she reached up, touched his cheek with featherlight fingers, and he was lost. His arms encircled her, his big hands fanning and sliding over her shoulders even as his mouth came down on hers, seeking, demanding, *taking*. It was as if a dam had suddenly burst inside him. Lost in a sea of sensation, Charity's body knew exactly what to do. She lifted her hands to his head, threading her fingers into his hair, pressing herself against him with a soft mewl. His lips were hot, velvety as they plundered hers, and she felt his tongue slip in between her open mouth, tangling with hers, tasting her.

She gloried in the feel of his body, hard and hot against her. So large, so much stronger than she, but there was no fear, simply a sense of being enclosed and protected.

And then suddenly, shockingly, he stopped, holding her fast, motionless, with arms like iron bands. Confused, her body still throbbing with unfamiliar sensations, she looked up at his face. His eyes were closed, his breathing ragged as he sought to get himself under control. At length, shuddering, he rested his head against the top of hers, murmuring her name softly. He loosed his iron grip and enfolded her into his arms. But the embrace was all too brief, and seconds later he set her firmly away from him.

'Forgive me,' he murmured, 'I…' Before he could say anything else, Charity touched his lips with her fingers. 'Please, don't say anything,' she whispered. 'Not now.' He stared down at her for a second, and she wanted to howl at the regret in his eyes. Then abruptly he nodded and stepped back.

'I'll be waiting for you in Stoke Fleming,' was all he said, before turning and striding swiftly to the door. He paused to check the landing was clear, and then he was gone. Seconds later, she heard a faint knock on her father's door.

As soon as the door shut behind him, Charity sank on to the bed, pressing her fingers to her own lips in disbelief. She could never have imagined in her wildest dreams that a simple kiss could affect every part of her. Even now, her whole body tingled with a strange restless need. She thought back to the regret in his eyes. Was it because he'd had to stop, or because he believed kissing her had been a mistake? There was no way to tell, but she vowed that as soon as they were safe, she would most assuredly find out.

∞∞∞

In the event, their departure from the Castle Inn was uneventful. The innkeeper was both amiable and courteous as he took their coin and wished them a safe onward journey to Plymouth. Nevertheless, as she climbed into the carriage, Charity's back prickled with a sense of being watched. It was only as the carriage quit the inn's courtyard that she felt her anxiety lessen slightly. Thankfully, a maid had thought to heat her foot warmer, and even wrapped in cloth, she could still feel the warmth through her boots. Closing her eyes, she leaned back against the upholstered seat, and hugged Freddy to her.

'How long will it take us to reach Stoke Fleming?' Percy was asking.

'Never been there,' Reverend Shackleford shrugged. 'According to Cardell, it's a small village about three miles from Dartmouth.' Charity opened her eyes. Clearly Jago had not trusted his real name to her father. 'Does John know where to go,' she frowned, suddenly concerned that the coachman might well take them on a wild goose chase.

'He says so,' her father responded cheerfully, his trust in the Duke's retainers absolute.

'Have you written a note to Agnes telling her we are delayed?' Charity asked. It would not be the first time her father had vanished into thin air without so much as a by your leave to his wife. And judging by the guilty frown on his face, this occasion was no different.

'What the deuce am I going to tell her?' he defended. 'I daren't tell her the truth in case old Jack gets wind of it. And, even if I could, it's not like she has anybody to call upon with Grace off in Torquay and Nicholas in London. And on the off chance she did actually manage to get a message to the Duke, or for that matter any other of me other sons-in-law, by the time they've organised a rescue party, we'll either be safe at home or in matching plots.' He gave an aggrieved sigh.

'Well, you'll simply have to instruct John in what he is to say,' Charity said firmly.

'You want me to tell him to lie?' the Reverend asked aghast.

'You lie all the time, Father,' she retorted in exasperation.

'I do not,' was his instinctive outraged response. In answer to her sceptical look, he added, 'I may have been forced on occasion to stretch the truth slightly, but only in the direst of emergencies. And anyway, that's entirely different to advising someone else to tell a plumper.'

Charity sighed. 'Very well, I'll tell him. And if we are not returned by the time Grace gets back ...' she faltered slightly. 'Well, as you say, we'll be home before then.'

The exhilaration she'd felt after Jago Carlyon's kiss diminished slightly as the reality of their situation struck her anew, but the coachman's sudden shout diverted her mind away from their predicament.

'I reckon that be your cull over there, near the 'edge,' he shouted down, slowing the carriage. Peering through the window, Charity felt her heart pick up pace as she spotted Jago standing in the shadow of a large oak tree. Seconds later, she was climbing down, her bag in one hand and Freddy in the other, shivering at the unwelcome chill as the afternoon sun began to dip.

Stepping towards the coach driver, she gave him the message for her stepmother, her voice gruff. As she spoke, she felt her throat tighten. John was their last link to home. Once he'd left, they'd be truly on their own. Ridiculously, she felt her eyes begin filling with tears, and she dashed them away with her hand, coughing to hide her weakness. 'Take care, John,' she finished huskily.

'Don' you be worrying yerself none, Miss Charity,' he responded, his voice equally rough. 'I know these lanes like the back o' me 'and. Grew up 'ere. Soon as I get back 'ome, I'll tell Mrs Shackleford, so she knows not to worry.' He paused, then leaned forward, adding, 'An' I'll be waitin' on their graces' return … just in case.' Biting her lip, Charity nodded and stepped backwards.

Without further ado, the coachman began the laborious task of turning both horses and carriage around, and five minutes later, he'd disappeared round a bend in the narrow track.

CHAPTER 14

Without speaking, Jago led them away from the lane, down onto a narrow-rutted track. Through gaps in the hedgerows, Charity caught glimpses of the sea, almost emerald in the waning light. After about five minutes, the Cornishman touched her shoulder and pointed to her bag, offering to carry it. With one arm already feeling twice as long as the other, Charity handed it over willingly. 'Where are we going?' she asked, picking her way through the deeper mud.

'Deadman's Cove,' he answered shortly, his eyes roving the silent fields around them.

'Now why does that not surprise me,' she commented, fighting the urge to laugh hysterically. When he didn't respond, she bit her lip, wondering if he thought her flippant.

'How long will it take us to get to this house of yours?' the Reverend puffed, balancing a bag in each hand. 'That's if I don't have an apoplexy or drown trying to board a boat somewhere named *Deadman's Cove*.'

Jago turned back briefly. 'Do you need to rest?' he asked without answering the clergyman's question.

'No, we're accustomed to traipsing the countryside carrying a week's worth of luggage aren't we Percy?' Reverend Shackleford wheezed. Jago hesitated, urgency showing in every line of his body. After a few seconds, he sighed and grasped one of the Reverend's bags. 'We have to be at the cove before the tide turns,' he explained through gritted teeth. If we're not there, the boat will leave without us.' Then hoicking the bag over his shoulder, he echoed the clergyman's sarcasm. 'I don't know about you, Reverend, but I would prefer not to be stranded overnight somewhere named *Deadman's Cove*.' And with that, he strode on.

After what seemed like hours but was likely less than one, they finally climbed over a large boulder and came out onto the coastal path. The only one not winded by this point was Freddy, who unlike the rest of them, seemed to be enjoying himself enormously. The Reverend sat down, fanning himself with the bottom of his cassock.

'We can't linger out here,' Jago warned. 'We're too exposed, and believe me, these cliffs are watched.' Hurrying them in front of him, he herded them down into some thick bracken on the other side of the path. The ground sloped dangerously towards the cliffs, and as soon as he was certain they were all out of sight, Jago again took the lead, working his way carefully down towards the cliff edge. Just when Charity feared they were going to have to use a rope to climb down, he turned to the left and revealed an opening.

The path down to the cove was narrow and almost impossibly steep, but somehow, they all made it to the bottom where a small fishing vessel was at anchor, hidden from prying eyes by a large pillar of rock.

∞∞∞

'Beggin' yer paddon, Jack, but 'e ain't there. I've searched every bleeding alleyway in Dartmouth, but Cardell's made a run for it. Reckon old Flynn scared the bastard off.'

'I said to kill him if he didn't talk.' Jack's response was mild, nonetheless more than one of the six men sitting with him risked losing control of their bladder. 'I want him found,' the gang leader continued. 'And I want him dead.' Then, dismissing the subject, he turned towards his right-hand man. 'So, who was the chit with the dog?'

'We're still lookin' Jack,' Will Dolby replied, his voice more confident than the others.

'Has she vanished into thin air too?' Jack's voice remained deceptively quiet, but Will found himself begin to sweat, his bravado disappearing. 'We'll find 'er,' he continued, struggling to recover his poise. 'Only a matter o' time, Jack.'

Jack stared at his henchman. Took in the beads of sweat now appearing on the man's forehead. 'You think we *have* time, Will?'

'We'll find 'er tomorro', Jack. Some cull reckoned he'd seen 'er goin' into the Castle. Remembered the dog. I'll be there at first light.'

'What about Mary?' someone dared ask, then immediately regretted it as their leader's eyes locked on him.

'We haven't actually *lost* Mary, have we though? We know exactly where the bitch has gone.' He gave a slow grin which terrified his men more than anything he'd said so far.

'As long as she thinks she's safe in Salcombe, I can take my time gutting her.'

∞∞∞

Charity sat on the deck, her head on her knees tucked as far into the corner at the back of the boat as she could. Jago had told her the back was not the back, it was *aft*. She didn't care what the *bloody hell* it was called, this was the first and last time she would *ever* set foot on a boat.

Her stomach roiled, and she wondered if she'd ever eat again. Especially fish. Jago had told her that putting something in her belly would help, just like he'd told her that standing and looking at the horizon would lessen her stomach's relentless churning. To be fair, he hadn't said anything at all when he'd swilled down the *aft* deck and handed her the bucket.

The worst of it was, her father, Percy and Freddy all proved to be excellent sailors. She could hear all three of them snoring loudly as they snuggled up underneath a filthy old blanket that looked as though it had last been used as a makeshift net. The smell obviously wasn't keeping them awake, but every time Charity caught a whiff, she had to stick her head in the bucket. Dear God, she hoped Jago's home had at least a scullery where she could scrub her clothes.

'How are you feeling?' Jago Carlyon's low voice came from above her, and she risked a glance upwards. 'Death cannot come soon enough,' she rasped.

'You must take some water,' he ordered sitting down and handing her a small flask.

Without looking at him, she took the flask and tipped it to her mouth. To her surprise the cold liquid, actually eased some of the rising nausea. She took another cautious sip.

'Are you cold?' he asked.

'Not cold enough to wrap myself in something like that,' she snorted, nodding towards their three comatose companions.

Chuckling softly, he climbed to his feet and came back moments later with a huge hand knitted sweater. 'Don't worry, it's mine,' he chuckled, draping it over her shoulders.

Gratefully, she snuggled into the heavy jumper. 'It's called a *gansey*,' he told her. 'Staple workwear for all Cornishmen since, well, forever.' He paused, then added, 'My mother made it for my thirteenth birthday.

The first time I went down the mine.' Charity glanced up at him, but his face was unreadable in the moonlight.

'Is she still alive?'

Jago shook his head. 'Consumption, nearly ten years ago now.'

'I can't really remember my mother,' Charity confessed softly. 'She died giving birth to my youngest sister, Prudence. She could tell he longed to ask her more about her family, but in the end, he remained silent. And truly, where would she even start if she wanted to tell him? She took another sip of water to hide her rueful smile.

She became aware of the fishermen's soft conversation. 'How do you know these men?' she asked curiously.

'I worked the boats in Salcombe,' he answered after a pause. 'These men have saved my life on more than one occasion.'

'Are they not afraid to risk Jack's anger by helping you now?' she questioned. 'Surely, they have families.'

'He does not know of my connection,' Jago answered. 'These men are insignificant. They slip in between the cracks, doing only what they must. If Jack were to try and put them all down, he'd have no time to smuggle anything.' His face turned grim. 'Oh, once in a while, he likes to demonstrate his power. A year ago, he had Fred's daughter kidnapped.' He nodded towards the larger fisherman. 'Sold her to pirates.'

Charity gasped. 'That's dreadful. What happened to her?'

'She died.' Jago didn't elaborate.

'How does he know it was Jack who took her?' she questioned.

Jago looked down at her. 'Because the bastard told him.'

They sat in silence for a while before Charity commented softly, 'Yet still they choose to help you.'

'They want him gone,' Jago answered matter-of-factly, 'and they know I won't stop until I watch him swing.'

Charity abruptly realised her nausea had almost disappeared, but she didn't want him to leave her yet.

'Do they know your real identity?' she murmured. Jago sighed and shook his head. 'I dare not take the risk.'

Before she could ask any more questions, the fisherman named Fred called, 'Ship to port, dousing light.' Instantly the small vessel was plunged into darkness and without thinking, Charity gripped her companion's arm. With only a slight hesitation, Jago leaned backwards, just enough to give him the space to lift his arm and wrap it around her shoulders. Face flaming in the darkness, Charity nevertheless leaned into his warmth gratefully. Fifteen minutes later, she was asleep.

By the time Charity woke, dawn was exploding across the horizon. At some point, Jago had laid her down on the deck and covered her with his gansy which was almost big enough to be used as a blanket by someone her size. Sitting up, she winced, wondering if she'd actually be able to stand. Her hair had slipped out of its pins, but there was very little she could do about that. Climbing to her feet, she tucked the errant strands behind her ears and looked around, finally spying her father and Percy standing at the front of the boat. Carefully stepping over the innumerable ropes and pulleys, she made her way towards them. Freddy was the first to spot her, giving a joyful bark in greeting.

'Finished casting your account, then?' her father commented cheerfully. 'I must confess, at one point, I thought you were heading overboard.'

'I'm feeling much better, thank you,' she responded through gritted teeth. Sometimes she wondered how her father had ever become a man of the cloth, given his distinct lack of diplomacy.

'Sea sickness really is the devil,' Percy added, his voice showing enough sympathy for both of them. Charity nodded. 'This is my first time on any kind of sailing vessel,' she confessed. 'I had no idea how bad it could be.' She took a step forward, then wrinkled her nose. Clearly, their clothes had been infused with the smell from the blanket they'd sheltered under. 'Dear Lord, I really hope we are not obliged to use a public conveyance,' she grimaced.

Reverend Shackleford frowned, lifting up his arm to sniff it. 'A good honest smell,' he announced with only the smallest wince. 'I'm persuaded the Almighty would not be offended at our stink seeing as it was gained whilst Percy and I were about his business.'

'In truth, Father, it's not the Almighty I'm concerned about,' Charity retorted. 'I'm more co…'

She was interrupted by the shout of, 'Land ho,' coming from behind them. And sure enough, the Cornish coastline began to materialise in the early morning light.

'Is that Falmouth?' Charity asked Jago as he walked up behind them. She couldn't stop her sudden discomfiture at the thought of sleeping in his arms earlier, and her voice came out slightly husky, much to her father's interest.

Jago nodded, leaning over the rail to gaze at the rapidly approaching port, the hustle and bustle of tradespeople already clearly visible in the early morning sunlight.

'We'll remain in Falmouth only as long as it takes me to organise our transport,' Jago was saying. 'I am known here, and don't wish my father to discover my return from another's lips.'

'Do you have a method of transport in mind?' Charity asked him.

Jago turned to look down at her, his expression impassive. Her heart lurched at his seeming indifference to their earlier closeness. 'My father has a small office on the harbour with the use of a horse and cart in case of emergencies,' he answered. 'It won't be the most comfortable journey, but at least we should get to Tredennick in time for breakfast.'

He stepped back from the railing, running his fingers through his unkempt hair. 'Please remain on board and stay out of sight until I return,' he finished, his tone wearily resolute, allowing no room for argument.

As she watched him walk away, Charity berated herself for her foolishness. What had she expected? He had far more pressing concerns than her, and it was likely he hadn't seen either his father or his home in two years. And she'd actually forgotten for a moment that they were fugitives. This was no May game they were playing. Indeed, their very lives could well be at stake.

CHAPTER 15

Barely an hour after dropping anchor, Jago had acquired the horse and cart, and they were back on dry land. As she climbed up onto the cart, Charity glanced back at the small vessel that had brought them here. There was no sign of the fishermen, and she suspected they'd chosen to make themselves scarce in the event their arrival had been observed by less than friendly eyes.

Within half an hour, the sea had vanished behind the rolling hills, though Jago had informed them Tredennick was no more than a mile from the coast.

Despite her aching limbs, Charity was fascinated by the landscape. It was very similar to that of Devonshire, but there appeared far fewer dwellings. Jago seemed lighter with each passing mile, and once or twice he even laughed out loud in response to her father's disgruntled comments. Even Percy smiled on occasion as he watched Freddy scout ahead, his excited nose either buried in a bush or high in the air, sniffing the wind.

As Jago promised, they finally arrived at his home around nine in the morning. As they rounded the last bend, Tredennick suddenly appeared, its austere grey stone almost seeming part of the land on which it was built. Charity gasped at the size of it. Jago hadn't warned them his home was the size of a small castle. 'Tare an' hounds,' her father muttered, 'I'm beginning to think there is much you haven't told us, Mr Cardell.'

Jago glanced over at the clergyman's frowning face. 'You're right of course, Reverend Shackleford,' he admitted. 'Starting with the fact that my name is not Cardell. It's Carlyon.'

Augustus Shackleford eyed him narrowly. 'Anything else? Do you have a title perchance?'

STARTLED AT THE QUESTION, Jago started to shake his head before stopping with a chuckle. 'Not unless you consider my father's honorary title of *closed-fisted tabby*,' he finished drily.

'Do those who work for him call him that?' Percy asked aghast.

'That and worse,' retorted Jago. 'Not normally to his face though.' He laughed at the curate's look of horror. 'My family owns Wheal Tredennick,' he explained. 'Tin and copper have brought us considerable ... well ... this.' He waved his hand toward the grey stone mansion. 'But in recent years it's also cost us significantly. As we dig deeper, it becomes increasingly hazardous to those doing the actual mining, and I've had many an argument with my father over his reluctance to spend the money necessary to provide extra safety precautions.'

He sighed before continuing. 'My sister's death caused a significant decline in my father's health, and he's been bedridden for most of my absence. From reports I've received, his deterioration has made him even more closed-fisted, and he's certainly not lost the use of his tongue. It's my hope that all the safety practices I put in place before I left, will still be in place on my return.'

Though she remained silent, Charity listened with interest. While Jago had told her some details about his family, much of this was new to her.

'Who's been running the mine in your absence,' the Reverend asked, 'if your father is confined to his bed?'

'My secret weapon,' Jago grinned. 'Richard Tregear, my father's estate manager, has been taking care of things. In truth, he handles my father much better than I do, and more importantly, we hold to the same moral standards.' He paused, concentrating on directing the horse through the open gates before adding, 'Though I suspect he will be happy to see me back. Even Richard's patience is not unlimited.'

Five minutes later, they were finally climbing down from the horse and cart. Charity felt as though every part of her had been taken apart and put back together again. Her muscles screamed as she hobbled towards the steps leading to a terrace fronting the large main door. Her father and Percy didn't seem to be faring much better as they shuffled behind her. Only Freddy appeared still full of the joys of spring, running around, sniffing and cocking up his leg. Charity smiled, his exuberance helping to lessen her anxiety as she stared up at the austere façade in front of her.

The dull grey stone gave the house a sombre air, though she imagined the flower beds along the edge of the terrace would provide a splash of colour in the summer. She thought back to the riot of wildflowers that covered the vicarage garden and felt a sudden sense of homesickness so strong, it nearly brought her to her knees.

'Are you well, Miss Shackleford?' Jago's comment brought her back to earth.

She blinked back the prickle of tears as she looked up into the concerned face of the Cornishman. 'Merely tired, I think,' she answered, truthfully.

At that moment, the front door opened, and all eyes were on the tall, thin man on the threshold. Evidently the butler.

'Thunder an' turf,' the Reverend muttered in a whisper that could have been heard in Falmouth. 'He looks like Death's head on a mop stick.'

'Father!' Charity admonished, preparing to apologise. Fortunately, the newcomer showed no signs of having heard them.

Jago, however, chuckled at the Reverend's assessment. 'Bennett's as deaf as a post, so nothing you say will offend him.'

'He looks … *ancient*,' Charity frowned, glancing up at Jago, then back at the skeletal figure, now tottering down the steps towards them.

'He's been here much longer than I have. He should have retired years ago, but simply refuses.' Jago shrugged. 'I suspect he'll simply keel over while serving tea in the drawing room one day.'

'You have a drawing room?' Charity asked with mock awe.

'We have two,' Jago responded flippantly. 'And a sitting room, a large dining room, a small dining room, a salon and a library.' He paused, thinking for a second before adding, 'Oh, and a ballroom.'

'I should love to visit your library,' responded Charity, still eying Bennett who didn't appear to have got much closer. 'Should we meet him halfway?' she asked doubtfully. At this rate they would still be here at lunch time.

'Oh, that would never do.' Jago grinned down at her. 'Bennett would be mortified.' She looked up at him. There was a lightness about him that had been entirely missing in Dartmouth. Clearly, Jago Carlyon was overjoyed to be home.

When the old butler finally reached within six feet, Jago finally stepped forward. '*Bennett*,' he yelled abruptly, making them all jump.

'It's good to see you, Sir.' The elderly butler gave a broad smile revealing a mouth suspiciously empty of teeth. Shuffling forward, the old man held out rheumy hands, which Jago took with obvious affection.

'Master Jago,' came an agitated voice from the doorway, 'Why didn't you warn us you were returning home?' A woman of middle years picked up her skirt and hurried towards them, yelling, 'Sam, bring the chair for Bennett.'

There was a slight commotion in the doorway as two young men, evidently footmen, came running out carrying a large Bath chair between them.

'Mrs. Penna,' Jago smiled, relinquishing the elderly retainer.

'You look terrible,' was her only response, before she turned her attention to the butler. 'How many times have I told you not to answer the front door, Mr Bennett?' she scolded, helping him into the chair. 'Take him round to the kitchen and put some brandy in his tea,' she instructed one of the footmen before finally turning back with a sigh and opening her mouth to speak.

Before she had the chance, Jago hurriedly stepped in. 'As you can see, Mrs. Penna, I have brought guests.' He stepped back as he introduced them. 'This, as you've probably ascertained, is our housekeeper, Mrs. Penna. She's our rock,' he finished simply.

'Don't think to charm me with your nonsense,' she answered caustically. 'When was the last time you ate?' Her sweeping glance made it clear she was referring to all of them.

'I thought you'd never ask,' Jago grinned. 'Lead on Mrs. Penna, my stomach thinks my throat's been cut.'

'Yes, well, I'll see to the young lady first,' she sniffed. 'Come with me, my dear, you look frozen to the bone.' Eccentric though the housekeeper appeared, Charity followed her willingly, knowing that if she didn't sit down soon, she could well end up in a heap on the cobbles.

'Take the hound to the stables,' Mrs. Penna ordered the remaining footman as she started towards the house.

'Certainly not,' Reverend Shackleford retorted. 'If Freddy is relegated to the stables, then Percy and I shall accompany him.' To be fair, the curate did offer a hesitant nod in agreement.

'Oh no,' Charity interrupted hastily. 'Freddy is part of our family. We couldn't possibly consign him to the stables.' She looked back at Jago.

'He is extremely well-behaved,' Jago lied obligingly, causing Charity to wince.

Mrs Penna pursed her lips but didn't argue, though she did mutter, 'Dogs in the house, whatever next,' as she resumed her march to the front door. The foxhound trotted alongside her, the very model of good behaviour. Sometimes Charity was convinced he could understand every word.

The entrance hall was very grand indeed, and Charity couldn't help gazing admiringly at the large glass dome built into the roof high above the staircase. 'My grandfather commissioned this house,' Jago explained, 'and as you can see, he had very grand ideas about how a gentleman should live, even though he was far from one himself.'

The glass dome ensured the large square hall was both light and airy in complete contrast to the outside. Ostentatious it might be, but Charity couldn't help but admire such vision.

'Do you wish to eat in the family dining room?' Mrs. Penna asked.

Jago nodded. 'If you see to some breakfast, I'll see to our guests.'

He led them to the right of the stairs, into a long windowless passageway. With only a few candles, it was exactly as Charity had imagined when looking at the exterior of the house. Dark, gloomy, and very spartan.

'As I mentioned before, my father does not believe in spending money purely to prevent accidents,' Jago murmured, guiding them carefully down the dimly lit corridor. A few minutes later, he threw open a door. Light flooded into the hallway as they stepped into a small, intimate, *delightful* room with a huge fire burning in the hearth. 'He does, however, dislike the cold intensely,' Jago added drily.

An hour later, the Reverend sighed and leaned back, entirely replete after polishing off a plate of bacon and eggs, toast and tea. 'That was most welcome,' he breathed, patting his stomach.

Charity popped a last piece of toast into her mouth and finished her tea. The roaring fire made the room delightfully cosy, and in truth, she could have curled up in one of the armchairs and fallen asleep. Freddy was already snoring in front of the hearth after finishing his share of the bacon.

Putting down her napkin, Charity wondered what they were expected to do next. Jago had excused himself almost as soon as he'd brought them to the dining room, presumably to visit with his father, and they hadn't yet been shown to any bedchambers.

'Where the deuce is everybody?' the Reverend questioned, after another ten minutes had passed. 'I'm done to a cow's thumb.'

'Mayhap they are still making up our beds,' speculated Charity. 'Mrs. Penna at least had no idea we were coming.'

'I think our arrival was a complete surprise to the whole deuced household,' her father agreed, going one step further. 'I hope the Master of the house is not one for throwing unwelcome guests out. I don't think my old bones would survive another night outside.'

'Don't be absurd, Father,' Charity snorted. 'This house is big enough to house twenty guests without them even bumping into each other. There must be a host of servants running it.'

'Then where are they all?' Reverend Shackleford questioned. 'And why is it so quiet?' He peered down at his pocket watch and added, 'Jago disappeared nearly an hour and a half ago.'

'Perhaps his father is too ill to consider us,' Percy remarked. 'Do you think Mr Carlyon might require our presence?'

The Reverend opened his mouth to disagree, then frowned, shutting it again. 'Mayhap you're right, Percy lad,' he eventually replied, 'but I don't see how we can simply knock on the old man's bedchamber door to offer our services when we don't even know if he's about to cock up his toes.'

'If you're referring to giving him the last rites, of course you can't,' Charity snapped, her weariness getting the better of her. 'And suggesting such a thing might well hasten the poor man's demise.' She shook her head. 'Mr Carlyon and his father have not seen each other for two years. They undoubtedly have much to discuss.'

Despite her declaration, Charity could not help but feel a little concerned. The length of Jago's absence did not bode well for their acceptance by his father. And they had nowhere else to go.

'Well, if I sit here much longer, I'll fall asleep at the deuced table,' the Reverend reasoned. 'So we might as well have a look round. If we happen to come across the master of the house looking as though he's not long for this world, we can at least put in a good word.'

Ignoring Charity's protest, he climbed to his feet. 'Come along, Percy,' he winked, 'let's do a little exploring.'

Muttering under her breath, Charity pushed back her chair. There was absolutely no way she could allow her father to simply wander around Tredennick without supervision. Goodness knew where he might end up. Gritting her teeth, she dragged the reluctant foxhound away from the fire and hurried after the two men, reaching the door, just as her father was pulling it open.

'Empty,' he whispered excitedly, stepping out into the corridor.

Charity rolled her eyes. 'You have no need to whisper, Father,' she declared, following him. 'We are in this house by invitation.'

'Which way shall we go?' Percy murmured after they'd taken a few steps. Despite her assurance that they had every right to be there, Charity didn't question the curate's continued hushed tones. Truly, the silence *was* a little unnerving.

'Mayhap we could head for the garden,' she suggested.

'I'm certain it's raining,' her father argued. 'It does so all the time in Cornwall.'

'Well, it wasn't when we got here, and you've never been to Cornwall before,' frowned Charity. 'So how would you know?'

'My grandfather was Cornish,' the Reverend defended. 'And they say once a Cornishman…' He gave an enthusiastic thump to his chest around the area he thought his heart was positioned, then winced.

Charity shook her head in exasperation. 'Perhaps if we head back towards the entrance hall, we might find someone to help us,' she suggested. The Reverend nodded and started back towards the faint light from the grand hallway, Percy at his heels.

CHAPTER 16

*J*ust as they were about to step out into the hall, the Reverend suddenly stopped and raised his hand. 'What?' muttered Charity, trying to peer around him.

'Who do you suppose that is?' her father responded, pointing to a tall, thin figure slowly descending the stairs.

'Do you think it a ghost, Sir?' Percy breathed.

'Are you bacon-brained?' the Reverend whispered back irritated. 'Of course it's not a deuced ghost.'

'He looks like Jago,' Charity observed as the man reached the bottom of the stairs. 'Could it be his father?'

'I thought Jago's father was confined to his bed,' Percy countered.

Reverend Shackleford narrowed his eyes. 'So did I, lad. And I have to say if that fellow *is* the Master of the House, he's certainly looking sprightly for someone who's about to meet his Maker.'

They watched as the man looked around furtively before disappearing through a door to the right of the staircase.

'I understood he'd had an apoplexy when his daughter was killed which left him without the use of his legs.' Charity whispered as they watched him shut the door.

Unsure quite what to do, the three of them remained in the corridor just back from the opening to the entrance hall. Ten minutes later, the door at the bottom of the stairs opened again, and after a slight hesitation, the man walked out, absently rubbing at his head.

'He *has* got a bit of a limp,' Percy observed.

'And in truth, I've seen better looking corpses,' the Reverend added as the sunlight from the dome suddenly reflected directly onto the man's pale features.

'He certainly doesn't look well,' Charity agreed.

'But why the deuce is he sneaking about his own house?' the Reverend questioned.

'How do you know he's sneaking?'

'Everything about him says *sneaking*.'

'He's not wearing boots.'

'Or a jacket.'

'And he's not supposed to be able to walk.'

The sudden sound of a door slamming made them all jump, and if they'd been in any doubt that Jago's father had no wish to be seen, his sudden look of alarm and hurried move towards the staircase quieted it. Indeed, his limp barely slowed him down at all as he swiftly climbed the stairs and disappeared along the galleried landing.

'Ah, there you are.' Mrs Penna's relieved tones came abruptly from behind them causing all three to spin round guiltily.

'Some guard dog you are,' the Reverend muttered to Freddy. Ignoring his master, the foxhound continued his campaign to win the housekeeper over, by wagging his tail and rolling over. Clearly, he knew who had control of the larder.

'We were wondering where everyone was,' Charity offered lamely.

Mrs Penna sighed. 'There's been an accident at the mine,' she explained. 'It's all hands to the pump when that happens. I've only just this second returned.'

'Is that where Ja... Mr Carlyon has gone?' Charity asked. The housekeeper nodded with a sigh. 'The lad's been away too long.' Absently, she bent down to give Freddy a fuss on the head.

'Anyway, where are my manners,' she scolded herself a second later. 'Your rooms are ready, and your bags have been taken up, so if you'd like to follow me.'

'Was anyone hurt?' Charity asked as they followed the housekeeper up the stairs.

Mrs Penna shook her head. 'By God's mercy, no,' she answered, holding her candle high as she turned left at the top of the stairs, the opposite direction they'd seen Jago's father take.

'Is the Master of the house very sick?' Reverend Shackleford asked using his best *I'm a man of the cloth, you can tell me anything* tone. Charity threw him a warning glance as Mrs Penna frowned.

'He's hardly left his bed since Miss Genevieve died, poor man. The shock brought on an apoplexy. At first it affected the left side of his body from his face down to his feet. After a while, he regained the use of his hand and arm, and his face returned to normal, but his legs...' she paused to push open a door at the end of the corridor. 'It's my fear he's not long for this world. That's why I'm so pleased Mr Jago's finally home.'

She walked through the open doorway and stepped to the side. 'Here is your room, Miss Shackleford. I do hope it's satisfactory. Mr Jago said to tell you he'll see you at dinner. We keep country hours here, so that will be seven o'clock sharp.'

After handing Freddy's lead to her father, Charity stepped into the room. She barely saw any of the furnishing, her eyes drawn immediately towards the large four poster bed. At the sight of it, a rush of exhaustion hit her, so strong that she stumbled a little. With a quick nod of thanks to the housekeeper, and a wave to her father and Percy, she shut the door. Less than five minutes later, she was asleep.

The sun had almost gone down by the time Charity woke, the last of the sunlight shining directly into her face. Climbing out of bed, she went to the window in time to observe the most magnificent sunset she'd ever seen. So much for *it always rains in Cornwall*. Jago had not been exaggerating when he said the house was close to the sea. She could clearly see the distant waves shimmering like sheets of molten copper, the sky above afire with orange and pink. Spellbound, she watched all the colours gradually merge into a single point, as the sun finally began its fiery descent into the sea. Until all of a sudden, it was over.

Sighing, she turned back into the room, and looked about for a candle, eventually spying two on the mantelpiece. Quickly lighting both, this time using the tinderbox provided, she stared around the room with interest. A large fire burning in the hearth ensured the room was pleasantly warm, and the furnishings looked to be of the finest quality. Stepping over to the wardrobe, she threw open the doors and grimaced at the two dresses hanging there. She had only three dresses and two sets of undergarments with her. It could not be helped that Jago had already seen her in her one and only evening dress.

A more pressing problem was the clothes' odour. She had no idea how long they were likely to be staying at Tredennick, and she'd worn her day dresses one after the other since leaving Blackmore along with the same undergarments. She'd have to see to getting them cleaned on the morrow or she would undoubtedly begin to smell more than a little ripe.

With a sigh, she pulled off her current dress and gave it an experimental sniff, grimacing at the ever-present stench of fish. This would have to be first then. Tossing the gown on the floor, she quickly stripped out of her undergarments and stared without enthusiasm at the small jug of washing water on the dresser.

She was just about to pour the cold water into the bowl provided, when there was a loud knock on the door. Swearing under her breath, she picked up her clothes and held them to her front, shouting, 'Who is it?'

'It's the maid, Miss.' A pause, 'And the footmen. Mrs Penna 'ad us bring you a bath.'

∞∞∞

An hour later, Charity pulled open the door to her room, feeling considerably better. The bath had been lukewarm but nice and deep, and the maid had left both soap and thick towels for her use. To Charity's delight, she'd also picked up the discarded dress and underskirt with a disdainful sniff and taken it away to be cleaned.

In contrast to the empty hallway earlier, Bennett was waiting in the large hallway ready to direct her to the drawing room, though in truth sleeping would be more accurate. He'd clearly been parked at the foot of the stairs in the hope that anybody descending would wake him up when they got to the bottom.

After giving the elderly butler a quick shake, she waited as he got shakily to his feet, resisting the urge to give him a helping hand. Despite it being only a little way up the corridor, it was a full five minutes before he stopped at the entrance to what looked to be the drawing room.

As he bent over in an approximation of a bow, for a horrifying second, she feared he would keep going, but in the end, he managed to right himself before tottering off back to his position at the foot of the stairs.

Entering the room, she found Jago deep in conversation with a small grey-haired man. For a second, she was able to stare at him unobserved. Seeing him in formal evening dress for the first time, his dark, striking good looks almost stole her breath. And then his eyes were on hers, and the warmth in his gaze set her heart pumping madly.

'Forgive my sudden disappearance this morning, Miss Shackleford,' he apologised as the footman handed her a glass of wine. 'Hopefully, you've been informed that we had an accident at Wheal Tredennick.'

'Mrs Penna told us,' Charity confirmed. 'She said nobody was hurt.'

'Not badly, no,' Jago responded ruefully, 'but I believed the measures we'd put in place...' he paused and shook his head. 'Enough. Clearly, my manners have suffered during my too long absence.' He turned towards his companion. 'This is my father's estate manager, Richard Tregear.'

'Miss Shackleford, I have heard much about you and your father.' The manager gave a small bow even as Charity's eyes flew to Jago's, wondering how much he had shared.

'Richard knows everything,' Jago answered simply, correctly reading her expression. 'I would trust him with my life.'

Before she could answer, a sudden commotion in the hall heralded the arrival of her father and Percy.

'I understand you hail from Devonshire, Reverend,' Richard commented after the introductions had been made. 'I'm from that area myself. Where is it you call home?'

Reverend Shackleford gave a loud sigh. 'Well, I think gentlemen that we've finally been brought to Point Non Plus, as my son-in-law is so fond of saying,' he declared, pausing before adding, 'That would be the son-in-law who is also the Duke of Blackmore.'

'You have a daughter married to Nicholas Sinclair?' Jago asked, his voice betraying his surprise. '*He's* the Nicholas you've been referring to?'

'My eldest, Grace,' Reverend Shackleford explained.

'Do you think it so preposterous that a Duke might seek a wife in a commoner, Mr Carlyon?' Charity interrupted, indignation clear in her voice.

Jago raised his eyebrows at her waspish tone, and Charity coloured up, fearing she'd entirely overreacted. 'Please pardon my astonishment, Miss Shackleford. It was not my intent to give offence,' he apologised smoothly.

'Are you acquainted with Nicholas?' the Reverend asked, giving his daughter an irritated glare.

'I know of him, certainly,' Jago answered. 'Some years ago, he showed an interest in investing in Wheal Tredennick. Unfortunately, his terms were not to my father's liking.'

'Currently, he is in London,' the Reverend went on. 'I had thought to try and get word to him but feared that by the time he received my message, we'd either be dead in our beds or the whole smoky business finished with.'

Jago nodded thoughtfully. 'While naturally I would welcome the aid of a powerful man such as the Duke,' he said carefully, 'there are other, equally powerful men who are involved in the smuggling trade up to their treacherous necks. I do not think it would behove the Duke of Blackmore to come to their attention.' He paused before adding, 'Unless it becomes a life-or-death situation.'

'By then it might be too late,' blurted Percy. Nicholas Sinclair was only very slightly lower than God in the curate's eyes, and he was inclined to believe that the Duke could solve every problem short of death.

'Let us continue this discussion over dinner,' Jago suggested, noting the footman hovering on the threshold. 'Miss Shackleford?' He held out his arm courteously and Charity bit her lip, wanting to apologise for her outburst. In the end, she managed a contrite smile and took his proffered arm.

The corridor leading to the dining room was much easier to negotiate without risking life and limb this time round as the candles in the wall sconces had been lit, casting a warm glow over the gloomy passageway. Charity gave a sigh of relief. At least Jago's father did not expect them to find their way in the pitch black.

'Is your father aware of our presence?' she couldn't help but ask as she was shown to a seat at the dining table.

Jago cast her a rueful glance from under his lids. 'Yes he's aware,' he conceded, taking his own seat. 'Though with his health as it is, I admit to being sparing with the truth. He does, however, know we are close to unmasking my sister's murderer.'

Charity shared a quick glance with her father as he took his own seat.

'I can't deny I am glad of Jago's return,' commented Richard as the first course was brought in. 'I think I speak for everyone at Tredennick when I say he's been sorely missed.'

Jago waited until the footmen had finished serving their soup and shut the dining room door behind them before speaking.

'My father aside,' he said, helping himself to a piece of bread, 'we must focus all our efforts on bringing the madman behind the Hope Cove gang to justice before he gets wind of our knowledge and goes to ground.' He looked round the table, his gaze finally settling on Percy. 'I understand your desire to involve the Duke,' he admitted, 'but we do not have the time. Were his grace in Devon, things might be different, but London is a whole world away. We must needs deal with this ourselves.'

'Do you seek to bring Jack down to ease your own guilt?' Reverend Shackleford asked brusquely. 'Forgive my bluntness, but my daughter's life is at stake, and I wish to know that you have her safety as your predominant concern.'

'Father!' Charity protested, her face pink.

'You have my word,' Jago answered without hesitation. 'Bringing retribution to the man who killed my sister has been my sole motivation for too long. I need to see this finished.' His voice became suddenly rough as he added, 'But I will do nothing that might put your daughter's life in danger.'

The Reverend nodded, seemingly satisfied. 'So, what is the plan?' he asked.

'I have an associate in the Falmouth Customs office who has been following my progress,' Jago confessed. 'He's ambitious, but honest and sees his best chance for advancement is by putting a stop to the Hope Cove gang's murderous activities.' He paused and took a large sip of his wine.

'Not long after Genevieve's death, we were on the cut. Nursing our grievances the way only drunken fools do. I ended up telling him my suspicions about my sister's killer. The next day he came here to see me. Asked me if I'd be interested in putting a rub in the way of Jack's plans. When I said yes, he gave me an identity and put me in contact with a fisherman in Salcombe. Richard agreed to run the mine, and I went with my father's blessing.' He shook his head. 'Neither of us had any idea we'd still be trying to put an end to the varlet nearly two years later.

'As yet he is not aware that we finally have Jack's identity. Tomorrow, Reverend, you and I will go to his office and give a full accounting of what has happened.'

'What about Percy?' Reverend Shackleford asked, ignoring the curate's look of alarm. 'Don't you want his version?'

'I don't believe that including Mary Noon in our account will add anything of worth,' Jago responded evenly. 'And I assume Percy would prefer his mother to be kept out of events?' He turned to the curate who stammered his thanks.

'What about me?' Charity burst out. 'I'm the one who identified him.' Unfortunately before Jago could respond, there was a knock at the door as the main course was brought in, causing Charity to grind her teeth together in silent frustration. Truly, keeping quiet was not one of her strong points.

'Yes, you are,' conceded Jago as soon as the door was again closed, 'and once I reveal Jack's real identity, it's my hope that Falmouth Customs officers are far enough removed to relish the thought of bringing the Hope Cove gang down. But we cannot guarantee that *none* will be in Jack's employ and consequently wish you dead.'

'But if his identity becomes common knowledge, how would Miss Shackleford's death serve?' quizzed Richard.

'We can't afford to let that happen. If Jack gets wind that his identity has been revealed, he'll simply go to ground. The smuggling ring must be caught in the act and Jack with them. Follow Jack and we catch them red-handed.' Jago looked over at Charity, adding, 'If he has the chance to go into hiding, he will do everything he can to see you dead.'

'So who is this deuced rogue in real life?' the Reverend demanded.

'His name is George Barnet. As Miss Shackleford discovered, he owns a local butchery business. Well liked by his customers. Indeed, the very last man you'd expect to be involved in such heinous activities. But underneath it all, our Mr Barnet is a butcher in every sense of the word.'

CHAPTER 17

The next morning, her father and Jago Carlyon were gone just after dawn. Having tossed and turned for the majority of the night, Charity was awake when her father knocked softly, asking to leave Freddy with her. Truly she was glad of his furry company, and it was only after snuggling the foxhound to her that she finally slept.

She awoke to another knock on the door, this time from the maid who had brought some warm water for washing. 'It's another beautiful day, Miss,' she smiled as she placed the water on the dresser and pulled open the heavy drapes covering the window. The sudden influx of light flooding into the room had Charity squinting and covering her eyes.

'Can I bring you some breakfast, Miss?' the maid asked.

'What time is it?' Charity asked, her voice still groggy from sleep.

'Half past ten, Miss,' was the cheery response.

Charity sat up in alarm. Truly she'd never slept so late. At the vicarage, she and Chastity were seldom abed after eight.

The thought of her sister brought on an abrupt pang of loneliness. Of late, irritation with her twin had overtaken affection, and Charity suddenly gasped as remorse slammed into her. She would give a King's ransom to have her sister with her now.

Realising the maid was waiting for her answer, Charity shook her head. 'I'll come down for breakfast,' she decided, making an effort to smile.

The maid nodded her head in return and gave a small bob. 'It'll be served in the morning room, Miss,' she added before shutting the door.

Half an hour later, she was heading out of the front door with Freddy in tow. Originally intending to simply let the foxhound do his business, she found the weather so clement, she elected to take a short walk instead. Breakfast could wait.

Reluctant to get her boots muddy, she wandered along the large terrace towards the side of the house while Freddy sniffed his way alongside her. To her right, the distant sea sparkled and shone in the sunlight. As she turned the corner, she realised that the terrace circled round to the back of the house, so she continued her stroll. The view from the back was just as stunning, though here the waves were replaced by wild moorland, a carpet of gorse already covering the hills in a bloom of yellow.

What would it be like to live in such a place? The thought came unbidden, and with it an image of her and Jago taking breakfast together. Foolishly perhaps, she allowed her daydreams to continue. Picturing them sitting on this very terrace, children playing on the lawn beyond. Would Jago ever consider her as a wife? Indeed, would she want him to? It was a long way from Blackmore and her sister. She gave a small rueful chuckle. In truth, it was a long way from *anywhere*.

Pausing, she looked up at the house and tried to imagine what it would be like to live within its dour stone walls. Suddenly, her attention was drawn to a first-floor window. There was a man sitting in front of it. Morgan Carlyon. As soon as he realised he'd been spotted, he put down his head, but not before she saw his expression. With a sudden chill, she understood that whatever feelings Jago might hold for her, he would never receive his father's blessing.

No longer taking in the scenery, her mind a whirl, she continued her stroll. Why would Jago's father harbour such a dislike for her? And she was entirely certain, despite their eyes meeting all too briefly, that the look in his eyes had been just that. *Intense* dislike. Almost hatred. Suddenly cold, she hugged her cloak to her and increased her pace.

There was something about Morgan Carlyon. Something other than the fact he was hiding the extent of his disabilities from his family, and possibly everyone. Mayhap he was simply afraid of losing his only remaining child.

Charity shook her head. Such speculation would get her nowhere. Indeed, she could not say for sure whether Jago had any feelings for her at all. He'd kissed her yes, and she believed the look in his eyes had held something more than simple lust. But when all's said and done, she'd never been kissed by anyone else so had no yardstick to measure it by.

And for that matter, what the deuce did it matter? They must needs focus all their efforts on stopping the murderous George Barnet in his tracks. Anything else would simply have to wait.

Calling Freddy to her, Charity hurried round the far side of the house, eventually returning to the front. Above her, the sun had gone behind a large black cloud, casting a dark shadow over the terrace. Glancing up, she felt her stomach tighten and shied away from the sudden fear that it could be an omen.

Charity was directed to the morning room by a cheerful footman. Once inside, she'd never been more grateful to see her father's curate. Percy was already seated, enthusiastically ploughing his way through a large plate of ham and eggs.

'Did you sleep well?' Charity asked, picking up her napkin and giving a smiling nod to the maid's offer of freshly carved ham and boiled eggs.

'Yes indeed, Miss Charity,' the curate responded. 'I must admit since coming here, I have felt a lightness of spirit previously missing in Dartmouth…' he trailed off, and Charity guessed that the missing part of his sentence was concerning the presence of his mother. She felt sorry for Percy but couldn't help wondering how such a timid, pious soul had issued from Mary Noon's loins. Mayhap Percy was more like his father.

Tapping her egg with a spoon, she found herself unaccountably hungry, and for the next few minutes, she concentrated on her breakfast, keeping her thoughts determinedly away from Jago Carlyon by thinking about Percy's family.

'Was your father a fisherman?' she asked at length.

Surprised, Percy looked up from his second helping of toast and nodded. 'Lost at sea when I was a babe,' he clarified.

'What about brothers and sisters?' she probed, never having thought to ask before. Truly, Percy had always been part of the furniture.

'One sister,' he answered. 'She died before her fifth birthday. Ate some bad mussels.' He sighed and shook his head. 'Mother was never the same after that. Something broke inside I think.'

Charity's hand hovered between her plate and her mouth, her food forgotten as she listened. 'Why did you become a clergyman?' she asked when he didn't say anything further.

Percy gave a sad smile. 'When Lizzie died, I knew there had to be a reason. And not just a reason she died, but a reason for her being here in the first place.' He paused, giving his leftover toast to Freddy. 'In the end, I found it in God,' he finished with a shrug.

Charity stared at the small, skinny man with his familiar tufts of hair sticking out in all directions and wondered if she knew him at all. In truth, she'd never even tried to know him. Percy had simply *always* been there. She wondered if any of her sisters had ever questioned him about his family. Sudden guilt swamped her.

As if guessing the direction of her thoughts, Percy suddenly smiled. 'Please don't concern yourself, Miss Charity,' he said, 'I am very happy at Blackmore. The Reverend is like the father I never had, and all of you...' He paused and actually chuckled. 'Well, I could not have asked for a more *interesting* family.'

Charity gazed at the curate open mouthed. She'd learned more about him in ten minutes than she had in eighteen years. Including the fact that he actually had a sense of humour. She grinned back, her self-reproach, while not gone entirely, most certainly lessened. She vowed that when all this was over, she would do her best to ensure that Percy Noon's standing in the vicarage was never again reduced to that of a proverbial door mat.

'Would you like to pay a visit to the library?' she asked impulsively, remembering Jago had mentioned the house contained one. 'It's likely my father and Mr Carlyon will not return before this afternoon.' At the curate's eager nod, she pushed back her chair and climbed to her feet, calling Freddy from his chosen spot under the table. The morning room was directly accessed from the main entrance hall, and clipping on the foxhound's lead, Charity stepped into the huge space, looking round for someone to direct them to their destination. But while she could hear someone speaking, there was no one in sight.

Taking a step in the direction of the voices, she halted and looked over at the room on the opposite side of the hall. The one they'd seen Jago's father disappear into – was it only yesterday? A sudden idea taking hold, she abruptly changed direction, beckoning Percy to follow her. Seconds later, they were outside the room in question. Charity glanced over at the curate who looked back at her in perfect understanding. They were simply looking for the library.

Before she had a chance to question what she was doing, Charity grasped the doorknob and twisted. The door was not locked, and she was able to push it open quite easily. With a quick glance round, she grabbed Percy's arm and together they entered the room, dragging Freddy behind them.

Carefully shutting the door, Charity gazed around what was a mirror of the morning room. Only this one had black drapes at the windows, and everything was covered in dustsheets. It had undoubtedly been used once upon a time as a sitting room. The sun streaming through a gap in the closed curtains revealed it to be a pleasant room that would likely receive the sun throughout most of the day. There were two winged chairs facing the fireplace and to the right, a small desk. Behind the door, stood a narrow bookcase, though with its covering, they were unable to tell if it contained any books.

The room had clearly been someone's favourite, though evidently not recently. Stepping forward, Charity fought the urge to peek under the dustsheets. Even without revealing the furniture underneath, it was evident that the room had been predominantly used by a woman. The wall coverings were a soft pink, and the pictures on the wall depicted flowering gardens, apart from the one over the fireplace. Standing underneath it, Charity stared up at the portrait of a young woman. Her features were delicate, but she had the same honey-coloured eyes as Jago. Was this Genevieve? She turned back to look at Percy.

'Mayhap this was why Mr Carlyon came into the room,' the curate mused. 'To gaze upon the features of his daughter.' He shook his head with a sigh. 'Simple grief.'

Charity nodded, feeling suddenly uncomfortable at the thought of intruding upon someone's private anguish. Then she thought back to the furtive way he'd entered and exited this room. The loathing in his gaze as he'd stared down at her. And why was he lying about the state of his health? *Something* was amiss. She looked round the room again. 'Do you think he could have been looking for something?' she questioned. 'I mean, why the secrecy? No one would think any the less of him for wishing to spend time in a room that was clearly a favourite of his daughter.'

'What kind of something?' Percy questioned doubtfully. Charity thought back to Morgan Carlyon's hostile gaze. She hadn't shared the incident with the curate, fearing he would think her imagining things. Her father too would doubtless think her dicked in the nob if she told him about it. And naturally she could not confide in Jago.

Feeling suddenly alone, she looked down at the foxhound who wagged his tail in response. *Tonight*. Tonight she would return to search this room, bringing Freddy with her. The foxhound might not be much help, but he'd at least provide some company. She narrowed her eyes in thought, wondering what time would be best, then suddenly her thoughts screeched to a halt. What the deuce was she thinking? How on earth could she look Jago in the eyes, knowing she was snooping around his house? Whatever his father was or wasn't up to was entirely none of her business.

With a sigh, she declared that Percy was undoubtedly correct. 'Grief can make a person act entirely out of character,' she agreed, leading the way to the door before stopping and turning back. 'I think perhaps it would be best if we did not tell anyone we've been in here,' she suggested. 'After all, we don't wish to cause offense to the man who has put a roof over our head in our hour of need.'

To her relief, after giving it some thought, Percy gave an understanding nod. Charity just hoped nobody would have cause to ask him directly about it. The curate's aversion to lying was legendary, at least in part she suspected because he wasn't very good at it.

Carefully turning the doorknob, Charity eased the door open slightly and peeked round the crack for just long enough to establish that the hall was empty. Then giving a quick nod to Percy, she pulled it open the rest of the way and stepped out into the hall, Percy on her heels.

She had just managed to shut the door behind her when a sudden voice came from the morning room. 'Are you looking for somewhere, Miss Shackleford?'

It was all Charity could do not to jump. She had no idea whether Mrs Penna had observed them exiting the small sitting room, but if she had, to deny it would simply arouse the housekeeper's suspicions.

'Oh, Mrs. Penna,' she sighed, stepping forward. 'Thank goodness, you're here. Percy and I are looking for the library.' She paused, then took a chance, waving vaguely back at the room they'd just left. 'We mistakenly thought this might be it.'

'That was Miss Genevieve's room,' Mrs. Penna confirmed, walking towards them, 'but the Master doesn't allow anyone to use it now.'

Charity made a sympathetic sound, stepping away from the door. 'We thought so as soon as we saw all the dust sheets. What happened to Miss Carlyon was so very sad.' She waited to see if the housekeeper would give any indication that she was aware of the reason for Jago's two-year absence.

Mrs Penna's response was a regretful sigh. 'Aye,' she agreed. 'Things have never been the same since she went over that cliff.' She shook her head, before saying briskly, 'Right then, let me show you the whereabouts of the library.'

After a quick glance at Percy, Charity smiled and hurried to follow the housekeeper, this time in the opposite direction to the dining room they'd eaten in last evening. The corridor was no less dark than the one they'd already negotiated, but fortunately, on this occasion, they didn't have to walk far. Throwing open a door, Mrs Penna stepped through. 'Here we are,' she declared with a grand sweep of her hand.

Charity looked around in awe. This library rivalled the one in Blackmore. For a few seconds, she forgot her suspicions as she twirled round in delight.

'Miss Genevieve loved this library too,' the housekeeper commented sadly. 'Her father didn't approve, of course. Mr Carlyon is old school.

He doesn't hold with the idea of women improving their minds.' She frowned, lost in memories of the past. 'He should never have sent her away. Her behaviour might have been beyond the pale, but at least she'd still be alive.'

With a sad shake of her head, she snapped back to the present and smiled. 'Let me bring you both some tea.'

CHAPTER 18

In the event, the Reverend and Jago Carlyon did not arrive back until late afternoon. This time their journey to and from Falmouth was done in a carriage, which according to her father, his arse was more than grateful for.

They were seated this time in the drawing room, their chairs clustered around a cheerful fire which did much to ward off the late afternoon chill. Mrs Penna had brought them tea and slices of a delightful lemon cake which was apparently the cook's speciality.

Both men were in high spirits and confirmed that Philip Lander, Jago's contact within the Falmouth Customs office, had immediately sent a missive to an officer he trusted in Dartmouth with instructions to keep a watchful eye on George Barnet and another on Joseph Smith. Lander had also sent word to Weymouth, the home port of the *Swallow*, a Revenue Cutter with a well-trained crew of fifty men who would be on standby to assist the local Customs boat. The infamous Jack's days were numbered. It was only a matter of time. The aim was to catch him red-handed on his next run.

'Knowing they're well on the way to catching your sister's murderer will undoubtedly lift your father's spirits,' Charity noted.

'I'm unsure whether to say anything further to him until they've actually got Barnet behind bars,' Jago answered with a sigh. 'We're still a long way from finally putting an end to the whole business.'

Shaking his head, he climbed to his feet. 'If you'll excuse me, I have a meeting with Richard and will see you at dinner.'

As Charity watched him stride to the door, she thought how weary he looked. It was unsurprising really. He'd spent the better part of two years playing a dangerous charade while living hand to mouth, and since coming home, he'd simply resumed the running of Tredennick. She hoped they would have an opportunity to spend a little more time together. Things were coming to a head, and she was persuaded they would soon be returning home to Blackmore. *His father at least will be happy when we've gone.*

A few minutes later, Percy excused himself, citing the need for some fresh air. 'Take Freddy with you, lad,' the Reverend mumbled, settling himself more comfortably by the fire.

Charity looked down at the comatose foxhound and chuckled. 'You'll have more luck moving a boulder,' she observed. 'Don't trouble yourself, Percy. I'll take the lazy hound out before dinner.'

As the curate pulled the door to behind him, Charity found her thoughts returning to Morgan Carlyon. Suddenly restless, she leaned forward and helped herself to more tea.

'So, come on then, out with it, girl.' She looked over at her father in surprise. 'You've been stewing over something since we returned from Falmouth,' the Reverend continued, 'and you've not sat still since Jago left.'

Charity opened her mouth to deny it, then slumped back into her seat with a sigh.

'Has something happened?' her father probed with a rare show of insight.

After a moment's internal debate, she told her father what they'd found in the small sitting room and Mrs Penna's subsequent revelations in the library. 'There is something … off about the whole thing,' she finished, 'though I can't put my finger on it. Why did Morgan Carlyon send his daughter away? I thought she was simply visiting friends.'

'Well, it hardly matters why,' the Reverend frowned. 'He might regret his actions, but he didn't kill the chit.'

'Why is he hiding the fact that he can walk?'

'Mayhap he likes the coddling,' Reverend Shackleford mused. 'After all, it's an excuse to put the whole deuced problem in Jago's lap.'

'So why would he approve of Jago going away for so long?' Charity countered. 'And on such a dangerous mission? *Knowing* there was a strong possibility he might lose his only son as well as his daughter.'

The Reverend frowned. 'Vengeance is a powerful motivator,' he replied at length.

Charity shook her head. 'I may be chasing a bag of moonshine, Father, but I think there's something wrong in this house.'

'Jago will be aggrieved to hear you say that,' the Reverend commented with a sly glance.

'I think he believes it too,' Charity retorted, refusing to rise to the bait. 'He's hardly spent any time within these four walls since he returned.'

'I dare say he wants to reacquaint himself with his inheritance,' her father argued.

Charity shook her head, irritated at his entirely uncharacteristic obtuseness. Her father was usually uncannily quick to sniff out a mystery, and entirely incapable of letting it lie. She eyed him surreptitiously. It had to be said, he did look fagged to death. Mayhap this whole business was taking more out of him than she'd thought. Charity felt a sudden lump in her throat. Her father might make a complete mull of most things, but she couldn't even begin to imagine life without him.

∞∞∞

Jago stared down at the letter in his hand and frowned. He was sitting in the counthouse at Wheal Treddennick. What the devil had his father been doing? How had he managed to give such orders without alerting either him or Richard? Tossing the paper onto the desk, he leaned back in his chair. Nearly three hundred pounds was missing. The estate manager had only learned of it after intercepting a letter addressed to Jago.

During Jago's absence, all mail was directed to Morgan Carlyon after which it was distributed as necessary. Richard was accustomed to receiving letters pertaining to the estate addressed to Jago but only after Morgan had read them. This letter had arrived just as Richard was leaving the house, having left the sick man's bedchamber only minutes earlier.

Instead of returning back upstairs, to save time, Richard had simply tucked the letter in his pocket, intending to deal with it when he got to the counthouse.

According to the missive, this was the third such correspondence the family solicitor had sent. Neither of the first two had made it into Richard's hands.

'Have you spoken to my father about this?' Jago asked.

Richard raised his eyebrows. 'Given that Mr Carlyon had done his utmost to keep the knowledge to himself, I thought it better to wait until you returned home.'

'And what if the whole bloody business had kept me away even longer?' he questioned.

'I would have found a way to contact you,' Richard insisted.

'I'm going to have to tackle him about it,' Jago grated. 'Can you make me an appointment with Cuthberts as soon as possible?' he added, referring to the Falmouth solicitors the Carlyon family had used since his grandfather's time. The estate manager nodded. 'God's teeth, I was so looking forward to coming home with good news,' Jago said, his voice cracking. 'I thought knowing that Jack's identity had been discovered would hearten him. But he showed no bloody emotion whatsoever.'

He shook his head, stood up and went to pour them both a brandy. Handing one to Richard, he continued, 'He was always a hard, contrary bastard, but now it's as if he's made from bloody stone.' Jago swallowed the brandy in one go, relishing the burning sensation as the fiery spirit made its way down to his gut.

After pouring himself another, he picked up the letter again. 'Whatever my father's up to, I won't allow him to get away with it, invalid or no,' he ground out, placing the missive in the bottom drawer of his desk and locking it decisively.

Richard raised his glass in salute. 'Here's to cutting through the gammon,' he murmured, swallowing his brandy before adding, 'Bloody hell, Jago, I'm glad you're back.'

Jago found himself giving a dark chuckle. 'You've spent too long toadying up to him, my friend. At least in my absence, you've had a taste of the real Morgan Carlyon.' Finishing his brandy, Jago glanced down at his watch. 'I need to leave if I'm to get back for dinner. Are you favouring us with your company tonight?'

'No. I wouldn't want to provide you with too much competition,' Richard grinned.

'Duly noted,' Jago responded drily, shrugging on his jacket.

'She's very attractive,' Richard persisted. Jago looked over in irritation, then sighed. 'Yes, she is, and believe me, if we'd met in different circumstances…' He left the sentence hanging as he snuffed out the candles, casting the room into shadow.

'But now this Barnet's as good as finished,' the estate manager persisted, 'her safety's all but assured.' He paused before adding, 'And you deserve some happiness Jago.'

Jago gave a rude snort as he followed Richard out of the door. 'I'm not sure I'd subject my worst enemy to my father,' he commented. 'And in truth, what's the likelihood of Miss Shackleford wishing to settle in the wilds of Cornwall, so far away from her family? Especially since one of them is a bloody Duke.'

'Love has no borders,' Richard quipped, untying his horse.

'I'm not going to dignify that with a response,' Jago retorted, climbing on the back of his own mount. As the stallion danced in eagerness, he suddenly had a thought.

'What happened to Stefan Petrock?' he queried. 'I noticed his cottage is empty.'

'Up and left just after you went,' Richard answered, struggling to hold his own mount back. 'The lads reckoned he decided to seek work over in Devonshire. He had a woman there apparently.'

Jago grimaced and shook his head. 'That's a damn shame. Stefan could have made foreman if he'd put his mind to it.' Then lifting his hand in farewell, he allowed the horse to have his head, trusting the stallion to find his way home.

∞∞∞

George Barnet, otherwise known as Jack, sat in the Seven Stars Inn and brooded into his ale. Three days since both Jago Cardell and the bitch with the dog had vanished off the face of the earth. In Jack's book, that was no coincidence.

He thought back to the chit's expression when she'd looked at him. Surprise, then fear, swiftly covered up by polite indifference. She'd recognised him alright. But where the devil from? He prided himself on his sharp wit and excellent memory. Nothing got past him.

But he couldn't remember ever seeing the woman before.

The door opened with a blast of frigid air, and looking up, he spied Will Dolby threading his way through the crowd. 'She was stayin' in the Castle,' he confirmed as he reached the gang leader's table, 'along with two gents - Charlie reckoned one of 'em was 'er da.'

'Was?' Jack interrupted briefly.

'Swears they left the same day she caught sight o' you, Jack. In a bloody la-di-da carriage. Told 'im they wus off to Plymouth.' He paused, ready to deliver what was clearly the key part. Jack eyed him irritably and waited.

'None other than Jago Cardell had dinner wi' the three of 'em the night afore they left. Charlie's daughter spotted 'em.'

'Was Cardell with them when they left?' Jack's response was quiet, and Will eyed him anxiously. Even in the dim light he could tell the expression in the gang leader's eyes was murderous. Nervously, Will shook his head. 'Though I dare say 'e might 'ave met up wi' 'em later.'

'You think?' Jack bit out. Picked up his glass and finished his ale. 'I want everyone on this,' he seethed. '*Everyone*. Find them. Bring them to me.' He paused, holding his tankard up for a refill. '*Alive.*'

∞∞∞

'What is it you like to do in your leisure time, Miss Shackleford?' Jago's question seemed innocuous, and Charity had never wanted so badly to be able to say she enjoyed needlepoint and playing the piano.

Unfortunately, she could do neither. Would he think her a blue stocking if she admitted to liking books? Surely not, since his library was extremely well stocked.

'I enjoy reading,' she declared, wincing as her voice came out more like a challenge. 'And walking,' she added hurriedly. 'Blackmore is exceedingly picturesque. When the weather is clement, my sister and I particularly enjoy the stroll to Grace's house.' As soon as the words left her mouth, she wanted to snatch them back. Why the devil had she dropped her titled sister into the conversation? She now sounded like the worst sort of snob.

But she needn't have worried, her father was on hand to remedy her blunder by dropping her into an even deeper hole. 'The last time you and Chastity *strolled* to Blackmore, I seem to remember you both returned with a bucket of frogspawn. Agnes swore there were tadpoles in her bedchamber.'

Charity coloured up, wanting nothing more than to strangle her insensitive parent. However, to her surprise, Jago gave a shout of laughter. 'It must have been fun growing up with so many siblings,' he commented a little wistfully. 'How many do you have?'

'Eight,' was Charity's tart retort, causing Jago to raise his eyebrows.

'THINGS WERE NEVER DULL THEN?' he teased.

'Anything but,' she grimaced. 'Indeed, it's a wonder so many of my sisters made such advantageous marriages.'

'Did they?'

Fiend seize it, she'd done it again. Did he think she was setting her cap at him? Or making it clear she didn't think him up to the cut? Charity felt like crying. *This* was why she balked against a Season. This constant having to watch every word that came out of her mouth.

'Your sisters have indeed been fortunate in their marriages,' Percy agreed as she sputtered, 'I didn't... I wasn't....'

Her eyes swivelled to the curate who continued serenely, 'But mainly I think because they all married for love.' He turned to Jago. 'A rarity in this day and age, wouldn't you say, Mr Carlyon?'

That was it, humiliation complete. There was simply nothing else to say. She actually found herself looking round for a convenient dark corner to crawl into.

'Well, I don't know about you, but I'm entirely done to a cow's thumb. My thanks for another splendid dinner.' Her father's interruption could not have come at a more opportune moment and casting him a rare grateful glance, Charity opened her mouth to agree. But before she had the chance to speak, Jago got there first.

'This may not be entirely proper,' he said hesitantly, 'but it is a lovely evening, and there is a full moon which I'm reliably informed is the first perigee full moon of the year.' He paused as his eyes locked onto Charity's.

'You mentioned earlier that you enjoy a stroll, Miss Shackleford, and I was wondering whether you'd consider taking one along the terrace? With me,' he clarified.

Charity eyed him suspiciously. His golden eyes were serious, but his mouth most definitely quirked at the edges. She turned to her father.

'I have no problem with it, providing you take Freddy with you and keep in sight of the house,' the Reverend commented jovially. 'When all's said and done, you've already spent the night together, even if it was on a fishing boat.'

Charity's face took on the hue of a ripe tomato. Had her father completely lost what few wits he had? Surely he wasn't *trying* to compromise her. She felt her heart give a dull, anxious thud. Mayhap he was simply desperate to get her off his hands. In truth, she couldn't really blame him.

'I will remain here to observe proprieties,' Percy interjected. 'Providing Mr Carlyon and Miss Charity do not stray far from the window, I'm persuaded there need be no cause for gossip.'

Climbing to his feet, Jago nodded to the curate gratefully. With the same baffling unconcern, her father waved a grateful hand vaguely towards Percy before shuffling from the room.

'Shall we?' Jago held out his hand.

Determined to show him she could behave with the utmost modesty when the occasion called for it, Charity took it with a gracious bend of her head. 'I shall have to fetch my cloak before we venture outside,' she faltered.

'I'm certain there will be one of Genevieve's hanging in the entrance hall,' Jago replied, 'if you don't object to wearing it, of course.' Charity shook her head as they stepped out of the drawing room. Looking back, she called Freddy to her.

Two minutes later, warmly wrapped up in a beautiful fur lined cloak, she followed Jago outside the front door into a moonlit wonderland.

CHAPTER 19

They walked in surprisingly companionable silence along the terrace while Freddy nosed about, chasing insects. The light from the full moon bathed the area in silver. Looking up in awe, Charity marvelled at the ethereal glow surrounding the enormous luminous disk, and behind it, millions and millions of stars, pin pricks in the blackness.

'It looks close enough to touch,' she murmured wonderingly.

'It's on nights like these that I cannot imagine living anywhere else,' Jago commented simply. 'I daresay you feel the same way about Blackmore.' Charity glanced sideways at him, wondering if he was merely indulging in idle conversation. To her surprise, he was staring directly at her, his gaze intent.

'It is not usually a woman's lot to remain close to her family after she has wed,' Charity responded carefully. 'My sisters are all at least half a day's drive away from Blackmore with the exception of Grace, but we are lucky enough to be able to visit one another fairly regularly. And of course we send letters.'

She paused and took a deep breath. 'If I should wed, it's my hope that my husband would indulge me by allowing members of my family to stay and agreeing to visit them in turn.' She stared back at him unflinchingly.

Jago remained stationary for a second. 'If I should wed, it's my hope my wife would allow me to indulge her in much more than family visits,' he countered huskily. Charity's heart hammered at the expression in his eyes.

'Would you be an accommodating husband, then?' she found herself asking, wondering at her boldness.

'When this is over,' he continued, his voice now a seductive murmur, 'it's my hope you'll allow me to show you just *how* accommodating I can be.' In the moonlight, his eyes had turned a molten gold. Her breath caught at the longing in their depths, and her entire body vibrated with an answering need.

Abruptly, a cold nose was thrust between them, putting an end to the moment. With a gasp of shock, Charity instinctively snatched her hand away, then looked down at Freddy who was gazing up at both of them, tail wagging happily.

'Good timing, boy,' Jago muttered drily, then raising his gaze to Charity, he added ruefully, 'It appears we've had a chaperone after all.'

∞∞∞

Lurking in the shadows of the landing, Augustus Shackleford waited until Jago had shut the front door behind him and Charity. Then, with a quick glance towards the drawing room to ensure Percy hadn't moved, he tiptoed back down the stairs, taking care not to allow his candle to go out.

Charity's question concerning the reason behind Morgan Carlyon's furtive visits to his dead daughter's small sitting room had played on the Reverend's mind throughout dinner, and now was as good a time as any to take a quick look. Indeed, if he left it any later, he ran the risk of coming face to face with Jago's father given that the dead of night was very likely the man's preferred time for wandering about on legs he told everyone were unable to support him.

With a last glance around the hall, the Reverend turned the knob and slipped into the unused sitting room. Once inside, he lifted the candle high and stared curiously around. He wasn't sure what he'd expected to find, but the feeling that this room harboured secrets became suddenly stronger. He found himself wishing Percy was here, though the curate would no doubt spend the entire time protesting about their inappropriate behaviour.

Reverend Shackleford placed the candle on a small desk, covered like the rest of the furniture in a large dust sheet. Wandering around, he lifted the sheet covering each piece of furniture and peered carefully underneath. There were no trinkets, no gewgaws that might reveal the nature of the woman who'd spent so much time here. The drawers of the desk were empty, and even the bookcase had been stripped of all its books.

Frowning, the Reverend looked round again, fighting an encroaching frustration. Perhaps Morgan Carlyon's reason for coming here really was to feel closer to his daughter. He picked up the candle, thinking he'd already been there too long, when suddenly there came the sound of someone turning the doorknob. Rooted to the spot, the Reverend watched in alarmed fascination, until abruptly the twisting paused. 'Can I be of assistance, Mr Noon?' called the housekeeper from directly outside the door.

Hurriedly, Reverend Shackleford crept towards the desk and got down onto his knees. There was hardly any room for a child underneath, let alone a grown man. He heard the knob begin turning again. Muttering an unseemly epithet, he snuffed out the candle and crawled into the hole, twisting himself around so he was seated with his knees up to his chest, sideways on. Seconds later, Mrs Penna let herself into the sitting room. Hovering at the door, she shone the light around the room, before making a satisfactory clucking noise. Slowly the flickering light faded as she closed the door. Clearly the housekeeper was making her nightly rounds, checking that all was well.

Breathing a sigh of relief, the Reverend listened to her receding footsteps, then, tucking the candle holder in between his knees, he tried to move. Unfortunately, that was when he discovered that his legs and arms were wedged so tightly in the confined space, he was unable to shift so much as a finger. Grunting, the Reverend attempted to lever himself upwards, with no success. Uttering a small moan, Augustus Shackleford rested his head on his knees in the horrified realisation that he was well and truly stuck.

∞∞∞

After Jago bade her a soft goodnight at the entrance to the drawing room, Charity wanted to whoop with sheer joy. She realised that despite their short acquaintance, she was falling in love with Jago Carlyon. Something she could never have imagined mere days ago. She couldn't wait to tell Chastity.

The thought of her sister was like a sudden dousing of cold water. Being without her twin was like missing a part of herself. And yet, if they both wed, the two of them would have to get used to being apart.

Bidding Percy goodnight, Charity climbed the stairs thoughtfully. Once outside her room, she turned to the foxhound. 'Do you want to stay with me or your master,' she murmured, stroking his soft fur. Wagging his tail, Freddy trotted on towards her father's room. Hurrying after him, Charity muttered, 'Traitor,' before knocking softly on the Reverend's door. There was no answer, and after waiting a few more seconds, she pushed open the door, sticking her head inside. To her surprise, the burning candle on the bedside table revealed her father's bed to be empty.

Frowning, she wondered where he could have gone. Mayhap he couldn't sleep and was even now searching for a book in the library.

Glancing back along the corridor, she wondered whether to simply leave Freddy to await his return while seeking her own bed. Truly, she was exhausted.

She began to open the door again, but clearly the foxhound had other ideas as he was already sitting outside her bedchamber waiting. 'So,' she hmphed, 'second best am I?' Freddy simply wagged his tail and preceded her into the room, wasting no time in jumping on the bed.

Pushing her father out of her mind, Charity began unbuttoning her dress, her thoughts returning to Jago Carlyon. She had no doubt that if he did ask for her hand, he would be doing so without the blessing of his father. Though the dowry Nicholas would bestow on her would surely go at least some way towards lessening his strange animosity.

Climbing into bed, Charity leaned over to snuff out the candle. Lying in the dark, she wondered what it would feel like to lie in Jago's arms, feel his big hands stroking her shoulders, her arms, even her breasts…

Shocked, Charity's eyes flew open, wondering how she could ever even consider such a thing. She'd certainly never before imagined what it would feel like to lie … naked with a man. But nonetheless, her rebellious mind continued to conjure up sensual images of them entwined together, until finally after what seemed like an age, she fell into a restless sleep.

She was woken by a soft knock. Freddy gave a low growl, then wagged his tail sleepily. Dazedly, she turned her head towards the window, but only moonlight shone through the gap in the curtains. The knock came again.

Muttering to herself, she climbed out of bed and shrugging on her robe, went to the door. 'Who is it?' she called, her voice low.

'It's me, Miss Charity, Percy.'

Frowning, she pulled open the door. 'Is something wrong?'

'It's your father. He's not in his room.' Staring at the curate's anxious face, accentuated by the candle in his hand, Charity felt an immediate tug of worry.

'What time is it?'

'Nearly one o'clock,' the curate responded.

'Mayhap he couldn't sleep and went down to the library,' Charity guessed.

'But his bed hasn't been slept in.'

Charity thought back to her earlier peep into her father's room. Clearly wherever he went after he retired from the drawing room, it wasn't his bed. Her worry became frustration. She turned back to look at the snoring foxhound. Mayhap they could use Freddy to find him if he was somewhere in the house. If not, they would have to wake Jago and organise a search party. Her exasperation turned into irritation. Where the devil could he have gone?

Then suddenly she thought back to their conversation that afternoon and her insistence there was something suspicious about Genevieve's small sitting room.

'I think I know where he might be,' she murmured. 'Hand me the candle.'

Seconds later, they were stealing down the stairs and Charity went straight to the small sitting room at the bottom. 'Why would he be in here at one a.m.?' Percy asked when she began to turn the knob.

'Who knows why my bacon-brained father does anything?' she muttered, determinedly ignoring her earlier intention to do exactly the same thing.

Reverend Shackleford was exceedingly uncomfortable. In fact he had a suspicion his arse might never actually recover, and he couldn't help wondering if he would be cursed to forever walk with a hunched back. Surely the Almighty would not be so cruel. But then the

BEVERLEY WATTS

Reverend thought back to his earlier reasoning for being where he was. No matter which way one regarded his actions, he'd most definitely not been about the Lord's work. And as Percy had insisted on more than one occasion, the Almighty did not take kindly to snooping, especially when it involved other people's property.

He could only hope that Jago's father would take this night off from wandering the house like a deuced ghost.

Sighing, he rested his head against his knees and eventually fell into an uneasy doze, only to be woken again by the sound of the doorknob turning. Lifting his head up in sheer panic, he cracked it against the underside of the desk and only just managed to smother a small groan.

'What's that noise?' asked Percy fearfully, hearing the sudden dull thud.

Hearing his curate's voice, the Reverend thought for a second that the bang on his head might be bringing on an apoplexy, until the shadows became defined as a candle was lifted.

'Percy, is that you?' Augustus Shackleford hissed.

'Father, where are you? What the devil are you doing here?'

Astonishingly, it was Charity who answered. 'I could ask the same of you,' the Reverend muttered, forgetting for a second he was being rescued.

The candlelight became brighter, and suddenly a face appeared at the entrance to his prison.

'What on earth are you doing skulking in there,' his daughter muttered crossly, 'come out at once you foolish old reprobate.'

'Are you completely bird-witted?' the Reverend retorted, clearly up to trading insults despite being wedged in like pilchards in a hogshead. 'Do you think I'd be here if I could deuced well move?'

'You're stuck?' Charity asked incredulously.

Before he could think of a scathing response, Percy's head appeared next to Charity's.

'What on earth are you doing in there, Sir?'

'What do you think I'm doing? Taking a deuced nap? Get me out of here.'

The two heads disappeared, and the candlelight waned as the holder was placed on the fireplace. For a few seconds all he could hear were mumbled voices, then suddenly, Charity reappeared. 'Right then, Percy will take a leg, and I will take an arm, and we'll endeavour to pull you out,' she announced.

Seconds later, his would-be rescuers got down on their hands and knees. 'If I'd known I'd be grubbing about on the floor at half past one in the morning, I'd have been more appropriately dressed,' Charity grumbled, firmly retying her robe. 'Percy, take hold of his knees.'

The curate bent forward. 'I'm not sure I can get in far enough,' he muttered, his left elbow almost taking off the end of the Reverend's nose as he tried to get a grip on his superior's knees.

'Ow, them's me baubles,' came out as a strangled yelp, seconds later. 'Are you trying to castrate me while you're at it?' the clergyman protested.

'Father!' Charity admonished. 'This is no time for obscene language. I've a mind to...'

A muffled 'Right then, I've got hold of his knees,' interrupted her tirade and she had to content herself with an outraged sniff.

'Give me your arm,' she muttered.

Obediently, Reverend Shackleford held out his arm. 'Bend your elbow,' she ordered. 'It will give me some purchase.'

'Are you ready yet,' Percy gasped from the depths. 'I'm feeling a bit light-headed.'

'Don't be such a chucklehead, Percy,' the Reverend grumbled, linking his hands and crooking his elbow. 'I'm the one likely to be walking with a deuced limp for the rest of me life.'

'Which might be very short,' muttered Charity, hooking her arm around his bent elbow. 'Right then Percy, on three.' Taking a deep breath, she ground out, 'One, two, three, *pull...*'

For a second there was no movement, then suddenly, the wood gave an ominous cracking sound, and the Reverend popped free, knocking both intrepid rescuers onto their backsides.

'Thank you, God,' Augustus Shackleford panted fervently.

Climbing to her feet, Charity gave a rude snort. 'I rather think the Almighty should have left you there for the rest of the night,' she declared, brushing the dust off her robe.

'Heartless baggage,' the Reverend muttered, wincing as he tried to get up. 'Give me a hand, will you Percy. At this rate you'll be carrying me upstairs.'

The curate sighed and pushed himself up onto his knees. Then bending forward, he looked into the hole the Reverend had just vacated and gasped. 'I think you've broken it, Sir,' he whispered.

Twisting round with a grimace, Reverend Shackleford groaned as he saw the panel of wood now hanging from the underneath of the desktop.

'Tare an' hounds,' he mumbled. 'Is there any way you can just push it back, Percy?'

'I'll have a look,' the curate answered, sticking his head into the cramped space. Taking hold of the small panel of wood, he endeavoured to manoeuvre it upwards. 'There's something blocking it, Sir,' he panted, tilting his head to the side in an attempt to get a better view.

'Can you see anything?' Charity's head appeared upside down.

Without responding, Percy, eased his hand into the exposed space and felt around. After a few seconds, his fingers encountered a small flat package. 'There's something here,' he grunted, trying to get hold of it. At length, he managed to hook his fingers over the object and flick it towards himself. With a rustle, it slid out of the space and dropped to the floor. Without stopping to see what it was, Percy gave the panel a good shove upwards and mercifully it stayed put. Breathing a sigh of relief, Percy picked up the small package and crawled backwards.

'What is it?' Both the Reverend and Charity spoke at the same time as they watched the curate turn the small parcel over in his hand.

Frowning, Percy looked up. 'It looks like a bundle of letters tied together with ribbon,' he murmured, handing them to the Reverend.

Charity hurried over to fetch the candle, and all three stared down at the small package, until the Reverend gave a small chuckle before murmuring, 'I'll wager these are exactly what old Morgan Carlyon's been looking for.'

CHAPTER 20

With fastidious care, Jack rinsed his hands in the chipped bowl. Truly, he'd have thought Fred would have learned his lesson after the business with his daughter. 'Don't kill him,' he ordered his second. 'Send him back to his crew. Perhaps when they spot the bastard's missing fingers, they'll finally get the message.'

The fisherman was hardly recognisable as he shambled from the small room Mary Noon had been imprisoned in only days earlier. 'Wot if 'e opens 'is trap?' Will questioned.

'He won't,' Jack answered shortly. 'Not if he doesn't want to end up swinging from the top of his mast.' He nodded towards the stumbling man. 'Help him up the bloody ladder, he'll never make it otherwise.'

After wiping his hands on a rag, the gang leader tossed the soiled cloth into the corner before taking a swig of brandy. As his henchman came back into the room, Jack handed him the bottle.

'So, why'd ye think Fred took 'em to Falmouth?' Will queried, taking a mouthful and passing the bottle back. Wiping the rim with his sleeve, Jack didn't answer for a second, then in a sudden fit of fury, he threw the bottle against the wall where it smashed, spewing its pungent contents all over the floor and wall.

'I don't know,' he said through gritted teeth, 'but by the time I've finished with Jago Cardell, the bastard will be begging to tell me.'

∞∞∞

'Who are they from?' Charity asked, unable to quite contain her excitement.

'Hold the candle higher, Percy,' the Reverend muttered, 'I can't deuced well see.'

They were seated in Charity's bedchamber having fled the sitting room as soon as they'd managed to get the Reverend off the floor. Fortunately, the clergyman didn't appear to have developed a hunched back, and by the time his two companions had pushed and pulled him to the top of the stairs, he was able to walk largely unaided.

Carefully, the Reverend undid the ribbon and allowed the letters to fall onto the small writing table. There were six letters in total, and all were written in the same spidery handwriting.

'Do you think we should wait until morning to read what's in them?' Percy commented after a particularly loud snore from Freddy, but after getting no response from his accomplices, subsided with a grimace, looking enviously at the foxhound sprawled out on the bed.

A few seconds later, Reverend Shackleford gave a sigh and passed the letter he was holding over to Charity. 'Your eyesight is better than mine,' he conceded.

Eagerly, Charity unfolded the missive and lifted it closer to the candlelight. 'Don't set the deuced thing on fire,' her father warned, earning him a scathing glance.

'It's very difficult to read,' she murmured, 'but it's addressed to Ginny, which I think we can safely assume is Genevieve … and…' she paused and bent her head, concentrating on her task. Suddenly her head snapped up. 'I think it's from a man,' she breathed.

'How do you know,' the Reverend demanded.

'Because his name is Stefan.'

∞∞∞

The next morning dawned bright and clear which Jago assured them at breakfast was entirely uncharacteristic of late February. 'Would you like to take advantage of the clement weather and visit Wheal Tredennick with me this morning?' he added. His question was clearly meant for Charity, though he made sure to include the Reverend and Percy in his invitation.

Charity, whose mind was still on their discovery of the night before, was torn between wanting to continue deciphering the contents of the letters and wanting to spend time with the handsome Cornishman. 'I thought we could take a picnic,' Jago added, thinking perhaps her hesitation due to the destination.

'In truth I'm a little weary,' the Reverend responded before Charity had the chance to say anything. 'With your permission, Jago, I believe I will spend some time in the library. The light is good in there, making it so much easier to read.' The last part was directed towards Charity, and gritting her teeth at the thought of having to hand the letters over to her father, she nevertheless gave a miniscule nod.

'How about you, Percy,' Augustus Shackleford continued. 'Would you care to join me? You can work on your sermon for when we return home.' He paused before adding jovially, 'In fact, I'm almost certain you could get three addresses out of the events of the last week. Four if you count the evils of drink.' Percy gave a thoughtful crease of his brow, then nodded.

'I would be delighted to accompany you,' Charity answered Jago finally. And any other day, it would have been entirely true. Still, she managed a wide smile as she pushed back her chair, declaring her intention of fetching her cloak.

Once in her room, she scooped up the letters, wishing she'd managed to read their contents the night before. Unfortunately, the lack of light had proved their undoing as the tallow candle finally burned down to the wick, leaving them in total darkness. Indeed, it was surprising her father and Percy didn't wake up the whole household by the time they achieved their own bedchambers, three stubbed toes and a narrowly avoided broken leg later.

Charity stared down at the bundle of letters in frustration, wanting nothing more than to childishly hold them behind her back at the sound of her father's knock. Then, sighing, she threw open the door and petulantly held out her prize.

'Jago will unlikely be around for afternoon tea,' placated her father, unable to hide his glee entirely, 'so we'll await you in the library to share our findings.'

A few minutes later, Charity went to pick up her old cloak, before pausing and looking at the beautiful fur trimmed one belonging to Genevieve. Jago had said she could keep it, and she was persuaded that the midnight blue colour did much to balance the boring brownness of her eyes. Truly, it was of much better quality than hers, and after a quick hesitation, she picked it up and laid it over her shoulders before heading downstairs.

Within half an hour, Charity found herself seated in a small curricle with a blanket across her knees. 'I did not think to ask if you ride,' Jago apologised as he navigated out of the driveway. 'However, the road to Wheal Tredennick is very picturesque even if it is a little longer.'

'In truth, neither I, nor any of my sisters ride well,' Charity admitted, 'though perhaps it would behove me to learn.'

'The track along the cliffs is not for a novice,' Jago admitted, 'It would all too easy to be cast onto the rocks below if the horse was spooked and you didn't have absolute control.'

Charity shuddered. 'Then mayhap I will be content with learning to drive a curricle,' she quipped. 'Indeed, if you'd observed my efforts on a horse up to now, you'd undoubtedly agree.'

The rest of the drive was so enjoyable, Charity forgot entirely about letters and mysteries. Instead, she found herself regaling Jago with tales of her unconventional family. By the time she got to the part about Queen Charlotte's unfortunate accident in the duck pond at Hope's wedding, the Cornishman begged her to stop, his mirth such that he was entirely certain his sides were about to rupture.

Laughing with him, Charity wondered at the ease with which she'd revealed the warts and all details about her family, but it was her fervent hope that one day soon, Jago would be able to lay his sister to rest and move on with his life. And if that life was ever to include her, there could be no secrets between them.

In the end it took them nearly an hour to get to the mine via the road, though Charity was convinced that calling the rutted track such was someone's idea of a jest. In truth, it was as beautiful as Jago had said. The Cornish coastline was magnificent – much more dramatic than that of South Devon. She'd been told that the north Devon coast had a similar ruggedness but had yet to see it for herself. Finally, coming round a sharp bend in the hills, Charity beheld Wheal Tredennick in all its glory. 'I had not thought it so big,' she breathed in surprise.

'We hold our own,' Jago commented, pride evident in his voice as he guided the horses towards the cluster of buildings surrounding the engine house.

Finally bringing the curricle to a stop, he hopped down and went round to help her alight. As he lifted her down effortlessly, his big hands encircling her waist, Charity was suddenly reminded of the erotic fantasies she'd indulged in the night before. Unable to stop it, her face suffused with colour. As she slid down his hard length, it was as if he could read her thoughts. For the next few seconds, the world and everyone in it disappeared, leaving only the two of them.

'Thank you,' Charity muttered finally, her voice husky. Before Jago could respond, a gruff voice hailed him.

'Mr Carlyon, din't think to see you 'ere today. And a guest too. How 'onoured is we?'

The sarcasm in the voice was good natured, and Jago did not appear to take offence. 'What are you doing loitering up top, Jori? Aren't you supposed to be digging up my retirement fund?'

'Reckon ye'll be diggin' yer own bloody grave afor that 'appens,' came the chuckled retort.

Jago grinned and turned back to Charity. 'This rascal is Jori Magor, my chief foreman,' he explained.

'Pleased te meet yer,' nodded the foreman, removing his cap.

'Have you seen Richard?' Jago probed.

'Meking me way there now,' Jori answered. 'Shall I tell 'im 'is lord an' master's askin' fer 'im.'

Jago shook his head. 'Just tell him I've left what he asked for in the counthouse.'

WITH A LAST WAVE, the foreman disappeared into a small building next to the huge engine house. Pointing to the massive construction, Jago explained that inside was the steam engine to pump the water out from the deeper parts of the mine. 'The building Jori just went into is the winder house,' he went on. 'There are cages inside to take the men down to the lodes.' He pointed to another, smaller building. 'The dry, where they get changed.'

Charity stared round with interest. The site was bustling, with a surprisingly large number of women and children. 'Do you allow women in the mines?'

Jago shook his head. 'They generally work up top, dressing the ore, cleaning, cooking and laundry.' He grinned down at her. 'Some drive the waggons. 'We call them *Bal Maidens* in Cornwall.'

'What about the children?'

'At Wheal Tredennick, they go to school.' He pointed to a low building off to one side. 'And when they're not learning their letters, they help with the washing, panning and sorting.'

Charity nodded slowly. There was much chatter and even laughter as the women worked, and she was relieved to see that Jago at least appeared considerate of his workers. Whether his father had shown the same care seemed unlikely from what she'd learned about the old man so far.

'I just need to leave some papers for Richard, then we can take our picnic somewhere a little quieter,' Jago was saying. Charity followed him towards a building behind the engine house, which he informed her was the counthouse. Even inside the small office, she could feel the vibration and hear the muffled echo of the water pumping.

A few minutes later, they were back at the curricle, where Jago unloaded a large basket. 'Mrs Penna is firmly of the opinion that I need fattening up,' he puffed, lifting the substantial hamper. 'Are you able to carry the blankets?' Nodding, Charity took the heavy woollen covers and followed Jago back through the hubbub of the mine workings.

'Can you see to the horses, Alfie?' Jago called to a small boy sitting to one side eating an apple. The boy jumped up with a toothless smile and nodded, running back towards the two horses standing with their eyes closed, clearly enjoying the sunshine.

Minutes later, the clamour of the mine faded as they approached the edge of the cliff. Jago pointed to a small, secluded beach. 'Are you sure you'll be able to carry the basket all the way down there?' Charity asked.

'I'll have you know I was the Cornish wrestling champion for two years running,' Jago retorted, hefting the basket onto his shoulder and starting down the steep path to the beach.

Busy tying the blankets around her waist, Charity didn't answer. Once she was certain they were secure, she lifted up her skirts and stepped carefully onto the path. Following Jago down towards the sand, her heart began thumping erratically, but not from exertion. She was entirely certain that when her father suggested she go on a picnic alone with the handsome Cornishman, he did not have an isolated beach in his mind as their destination.

Oh, she had no concerns that Jago would hurt her, or indeed force her to do anything against her will. She trusted him entirely. In truth, it wasn't Jago she was afraid of, it was herself.

CHAPTER 21

George Barnet stood on the deck of the *Swan* and watched as Dartmouth quayside disappeared around the bend in the river. The last thing he needed was an unplanned trip to bloody Falmouth just before a run. But some matters needed to be dealt with personally. And Jago Cardell was one of them.

He'd been so damn careful, building up the character of Jack. Keeping his two lives entirely separate. The few who knew his real identity were too terrified to reveal it to anyone. George had made sure of that. It hadn't been difficult. After all, butchering was his trade.

He was under no illusion that the rest of the Hope Cove gang followed him out of loyalty, but he *enjoyed* controlling them through terror, keeping them at each other's throats to stop them going for his. George gave a mirthless chuckle. They hated him alright, but their fear of him was stronger. And they liked the blunt too. Fear and money. The two greatest motivators.

And then Jago Cardell had come along. From the start there'd been *something* about him. Something different. But George hadn't been able to put his finger on it. Until last night.

Last night, he'd *felt* the fisherman's terror as he'd cut two of the bastard's fingers off. But when he'd looked into Fred's eyes, there wasn't just fear in them. There was hope.

Jago Cardell *inspired*. The bastard hadn't come to join him, but to bring him down.

George slammed his hand on the rail wishing he had Cardell's head underneath it. He'd take care of the Cornishman first, then he'd find and gut the bitch who'd given him away.

∞∞∞

Mrs Penna had packed enough food for a small army. As she popped the last piece of cheese into her mouth, Charity feared for a second she might burst.

They were seated at the foot of the cliff in a natural alcove that both shielded them from the wind and from any prying eyes above. Initially, Charity had struggled to contain her nervousness, but Jago's easy, relaxed manner soon returned them to the same companionship they'd shared in the curricle earlier.

Now, watching the waves lap gently against the shore, Charity felt a sense of peace, of belonging that she'd felt nowhere else. Not even Blackmore.

Jago had fallen asleep next to her, his large body stretched out taking up the whole of one blanket. According to him, the tide had travelled as far up the beach as it was likely to and would soon begin receding, so there was no fear of them being cut off. Still, she knew they would have to go soon if they hoped to get back to the house at an appropriate hour. But until then, the sun was warm on her face, and she closed her eyes, enjoying the unexpected heat.

After a short while, glancing down at her companion to check he was still sleeping, Charity surreptitiously undid the top three buttons of her dress, exposing her throat to the sun's warmth. Sighing, she leaned back on her hands and let her head fall back.

But unbeknown to Charity, Jago was not only awake but watching her through half closed lids. The sight of her unbuttoning her dress and parting the material to expose her slender neck and shoulders caused an instant hardness in his breeches that almost had him groaning out loud. Dear God but she was lovely. He shifted restlessly, trying to hide his arousal from her, but the very action drew her attention. With a small gasp, her eyes widened, then flew to his. The expression in their soft brown depths was his undoing.

She wanted him. Every bit as much as he wanted her.

Without thinking, he reached up and grasped her shoulder, gently, insistently pulling her down to him until she lay sprawled on his chest. Jago could feel her heart slamming against her ribs, but she did not remove her gaze from his. After a second, he lifted his hand to cup her cheek, then slid his fingers around the back of her neck. Slowly, oh so slowly, he drew her head down, down until her lips finally touched his. The barest kiss. But it was enough. With a groan, Jago lifted his head and plundered her mouth. Holding her head still, drinking from her lips like he was dying with thirst. Charity met him kiss for kiss, her mouth demanding, seeking, *melding* with his.

Slowly, she slid herself atop him completely, pressing herself against the hard swell of his cock. With a low groan, Jago gripped her shoulders and shifted, taking her with him. In seconds, she was underneath him, the lithe give of her body moulded to his. His head dipped to her throat, his lips and tongue seeking the bare flesh below the neckline of her dress. She gave an incoherent whimper and threaded her fingers through his hair, holding his head to the swell of her breasts, seeking … something.

With a growl, he fumbled with the remaining buttons, pulling and tugging the fabric aside, until her breasts were exposed to his molten gaze. Then his mouth was back on hers, capturing her tongue with his, even as his fingers cupped her breasts, his thumb strumming across her already peaked nipple. Charity cried out against his lips at the entirely unexpected, exquisite shock of sensation. Instinctively, she lifted her hips, grinding herself against the hardness between her legs. Then suddenly his hands shifted, his arms sliding behind her. She sighed in protest until suddenly, *shockingly* she felt his lips close over one nipple.

She shuddered at the exquisite pleasure of it, her hands clutching his shoulders as the sensation shot through her.

Almost mindlessly, she felt his hand shift, seeking the bottom of her skirts, then sliding up her calves, her thighs, beyond the tops of her stocking to the vulnerable skin above. Skilfully his hand caressed the tender flesh as his fingers slid in featherlight touches inexorably towards the juncture between her legs. Without even thinking, her legs fell apart, allowing him access to that most secret part of her. In fact, Charity felt she might die if he didn't touch her there, *now*.

And then he did. His fingers dipped, stroked. 'So hot, so wet,' he murmured, his voice hoarse with need. Helplessly she thrust her hips upwards, feeling herself slide towards a precipice. His mouth came down on hers again, his fingers expertly stroking, stroking. Restlessly, she shifted, instinctively seeking the hardness she somehow knew would give her release. '*Please*,' she whispered against his lips, sliding her hands between them, fumbling with the buttons of his breeches. He groaned as her hand slid inside and touched him, even as she bucked under his own questing fingers.

Dear God. Jago threw his head back as her fingers closed over him, his whole body trembling, on the verge of spilling like a green boy. She stroked him once, twice using the same urgent rhythm as his stroking fingers. His breath came out in harsh gasps as he nudged her legs apart with his knees and...

He couldn't. *He couldn't do this*. Not *here*, not *now*. His fingers stilled, sought to pull out of her wetness, but she gave a violent shake of her head, and clasped his hand, holding him to her. Her eyes flew open, and she stared at him. Jago felt her body tighten around his motionless fingers, and he realised she was close to her release. Gritting his teeth with the effort of holding himself back, he rubbed his thumb against the small nub at the entrance to her core. Once, twice and that was all it took. Watching her face, hearing her cry out as her release crashed over her was the most erotic thing Jago had ever experienced.

And then it was over. Her faced suffused with colour, Charity kept her eyes closed as he gently slid out his fingers and pulled down her skirt. She didn't move as he painfully adjusted himself and buttoned up his breeches. But when he sought to adjust her bodice, she suddenly pushed his hand away and scooted backwards. Keeping her head down, she fumbled with the buttons.

'Charity, look at me,' Jago murmured achingly. She gave an almost imperceptible shake of her head and continued to stare down into her lap, her hands now clutching and unclutching her skirt. Sighing, he leaned forward and laid his large hand over the top of hers, stopping her restless twisting. 'Look at me, sweetheart,' he repeated.

Something in his voice must have got through because she slowly raised her face. 'I'm so sorry,' she murmured brokenly. 'I… I swear I have never behaved so wantonly before. I don't… I haven't…' she stopped, tears spilling down her cheeks.

Sighing, he fought the temptation to kiss away her tears. God willing, that would come later, but not too often he hoped. Staring at her mouth swollen already with his kisses, he couldn't hold back a small, satisfied smile.

'And so now you think it appropriate to *laugh* at me?' Clearly the love of his life had recovered from her self-recrimination. 'Undoubtedly you are the wors…'

'Charity Shackleford, will you marry me?'

She sputtered to a halt and stared at him.

And stared.

Then, just when he was convinced he'd got the whole thing terribly wrong, she said, matter-of-factly, 'That's probably a good idea, and judging by my earlier performance, it would behove us not to wait too long.'

Then she threw herself into his arms.

Despite their intimacy, the journey back to Tredennick House was mostly silent. Charity repeatedly felt a hot flush of embarrassment every time she thought about her wanton behaviour. Who would have thought that she had within her a streak of shamelessness almost as bad as her sister Tempy?

Suddenly, she fought back a chuckle. The look in Jago's eyes had been most gratifying. She'd meant what she said about them not waiting too long, or truly, the temptation to sneak into her fiancé's bed might well prove too strong to resist.

'I would like to keep our engagement between ourselves until I have spoken to your father formally,' Jago suddenly announced into the silence. Charity looked over at him, abruptly afraid he might be having cold feet, but the sidelong glance he gave her was full of molten heat, and she felt her worries subside.

'I also wish to advise my father of my intention,' he continued before she had the chance to reply, 'but would prefer to leave both conversations until tomorrow, with your permission.' He paused, but she sensed he had something else to say.

'I have an appointment to visit our solicitors in Falmouth tomorrow and thought perhaps you, your father and Percy might wish to accompany me. Once my business is concluded, I will meet you somewhere for lunch.'

'I would like that,' Charity responded, glancing at him with a smile. 'Mayhap you will get the opportunity to speak with my father while we are out.'

'Is he less likely to give me short shrift in public?' Jago commented drily.

'I do not think he would do such a thing,' Charity answered. 'My father has many faults, but I do know he desires us all to be happy. If it is my wish to wed you, he will not say nay.' She gave him a shy sideways glance before finishing softly, 'And it is my wish.'

'There is nothing I want more,' Jago affirmed, 'but there is not only your father to consider. What about the rest of your family? As yet, they don't even know I exist.'

'They will love you as I do,' Charity responded simply.

Jago felt his heart swell at her words. 'I certainly hope so,' he returned huskily.

They fell silent for the last mile, but as he finally negotiated the narrow entrance to the Tredennick estate, Charity took a deep breath, knowing she needed to ask the question before they went into the house. 'What about your father, Jago?' she questioned hesitantly. 'He is yet to meet me. How will he feel about you taking a wife? Will he not think it very sudden?'

'If my father chooses to stay in his bed rather than be brought down to join us for dinner, that is his problem,' was Jago's harsh retort. Then he sighed. 'It's my belief that the apoplexy he suffered after my sister's death may have addled his brain. He is not the same man as he was before we lost Genevieve.' He shook his head before adding, 'He seems to have lost all empathy along with the use of his legs.'

Charity frowned, wondering whether now was the time to tell him that Morgan Carlyon was not as lame as he made out, but as she opened her mouth to speak, Jago pulled the curricle to a stop outside the house. He turned to face her and took her hand. 'I *will* wed you,

Charity, whatever my father's opinion. Naturally, I would like his blessing, but if he refuses to give it, then so be it.'

'What if he cuts you off?' Charity couldn't help questioning. Jago looked up at the large, grey-stoned building and shrugged. 'Then I hope at least one of your brothers-in-law will see fit to give me a job.'

CHAPTER 22

Charity grimaced at her evening dress, now beginning to look grubby and limp after being worn so often. It certainly wasn't what she'd imagined herself wearing on the first night of her engagement, even if it was currently unofficial. Shaking out the dress, she gave a deep sigh. How she wished the rest of her family were here. Then, she sternly took herself in hand. They would know soon enough, and that would be an excuse for another celebration.

Laying the dress on the bed, she wondered whether there would be time to get it cleaned before tomorrow evening. Hopefully by then, Jago would have spoken to her father and they'd be able to have a proper celebratory dinner.

Glaring at the offending garment, she had a sudden thought. They were going into Falmouth tomorrow. Mayhap her father would see his way into buying her a new dress. He would grumble undoubtedly, but surely he would not wish her to attend her own engagement dinner wearing a dress that was beginning to smell distinctly musty.

A knock on the door interrupted her reverie. 'Come,' she called, her happiness suddenly bubbling over.

Her smile faltered at her father's serious expression as he pushed open the door, Freddy in tow, and abruptly she remembered the letters and the Reverend's suggestion they meet in the library. Truly she'd not given them a thought all day.

The foxhound greeted her exuberantly, and Charity bent down to give him a fuss, suddenly reluctant to hear what the missives contained. So much had changed since she left this morning.

'Well, Charity, Jago's father is a piece of work, and no mistake.' He sat down heavily on one of the wingback chairs at the window. 'You'd better sit down, lass,' he muttered.

Frowning, Charity felt her earlier euphoria trickle away. Heart thudding in sick anticipation, she sat down on the remaining chair.

'The letters were to Genevieve as we'd surmised,' he stated after a moment. 'They were from a fellow who worked at the mine. Name of Stefan Petrock. Apparently, they were…' He paused, seeking a word that would not offend female sensibilities. He should have known better.

'They were conducting an illicit affair,' Charity finished for him flatly.

He nodded. 'Seems they were in love and planning to elope.' He shook his head and sighed. 'I don't think they had any idea how far Scotland is from Cornwall.'

'When was this?' Charity asked with a frown.

'By the dates, I would think it was not long before Genevieve was packed off to London.'

'So her father found out and put a stop to it,' Charity concluded.

'Am I telling this deuced story or you?' the Reverend retorted in exasperation.

'I'm sorry, Father, do go on.'

'Yes, well,' he hmphed, 'you're right as it happens. Her father did find out. Our Mrs Penna was the one who tattled on them, though I think she came to regret it. According to Stefan, she even went on to act as a go between. Evidently, she hadn't expected the Master of Tredennick to react so violently to the news, but apparently, his fury was a sight to behold when he confronted the pair. Not long after that, he sent Genevieve away.'

'Was Jago aware?' Charity asked, a sudden sick feeling in the pit of her stomach. To her relief, the Reverend shook his head.

'In his letters, Stefan begged her to speak with him. He seemed certain Jago would intercede. But apparently, she refused, not wanting to set her brother against their father.'

'So, the odious man sent her away,' Charity breathed.

Reverend Shackleford nodded with a grimace. 'Stefan's last letter declared he would be waiting for her when she returned. Apparently, they only had a year to wait until she came of age. Then her father would have no say in who she wed.'

'But she didn't come home,' Charity whispered. 'What happened to Stefan?'

Her father shrugged. 'I thought mayhap we'd ask Jago at dinner this evening. See if he knows anything.'

Charity didn't like the idea of quizzing the man she intended to marry. And in truth, she had no idea whether Jago would actually wish to learn about Genevieve's involvement with one of his mine workers. 'I have no objection as long as you do not seek to regale him with the sordid details of his sister's affair over the dinner table.'

'Do you think me entirely bacon-brained?' the Reverend declared indignantly. 'I might be occasionally lacking in manners, but even I would not think to inform a man at his own dinner table that his sister had been tying her deuced garter in public.'

As he climbed to his feet, Charity heard him mutter under his breath, 'I've enough of that going on in my own backyard.' She winced, thinking of her abandoned behaviour this afternoon.

'Come, Freddy,' he called to the foxhound from the door, 'there's still enough light for a quick turn around the terrace.'

As the door closed behind him, Charity remained seated, sadness for Jago's sister swamping her. She thought back to her father's muttered comments as he left and for the first time in, well, *ever*, she was grateful for his uncommon outlook on life. Truly, over the years, she and her sisters had made a May game of him.

But then she thought of all the times he'd involved himself in affairs that were entirely none of his business. He might not be completely bacon-brained, but still, it was generally conceded by everyone who knew him that Augustus Shackleford was no stranger to kicking up a lark.

True to his word, her father did not belabour the subject of Stefan Petrock, and waited to ask his questions until they were seated in the drawing room after dinner. As Jago handed him a brandy, he simply asked whether Wheal Tredennick's mine workers were content.

'In the main, yes,' Jago confirmed. 'I like to believe that we treat our workers with respect and care.'

'I can attest to that after my visit to the mine today,' Charity interjected warmly.

Jago gave her a grateful smile, adding, 'Most of them have worked at the mine their whole lives, and their fathers before them.'

'So you've had no one leave in the last few years?' The Reverend probed offhandedly.

Jago frowned, and for a second, Charity thought he was going to ask why her father was interested. But then he shrugged. 'One or two. Usually young men who are not interested in renting living accommodation and think they can get better pay elsewhere.' He took a sip of his wine, before adding, 'There was one man that came as a bit of a surprise.'

'Oh?' The Reverend did his best to convey polite interest.

'Stefan Petrock,' Jago mused. 'With our current foreman getting on in years, I'd hoped Stefan would be the man to replace him.' He paused, then shook his head. 'He'd seemed keen and was undoubtedly very bright. But when I got back, he'd evidently upped and left not long after I went to Salcombe.'

Jago frowned. 'It was entirely out of character, and I admit to being surprised, but according to Richard he decided to seek his fortune in Devonshire. Apparently, there was a woman.'

The Reverend sighed. 'Men will do many a foolish thing for love,' he declared. 'Why…'

Fearful her father would entirely put his foot in it, Charity interrupted with, 'Jago has an appointment in Falmouth tomorrow and was wondering if we would like to accompany him. What say you, Father?'

'Well, I have no objections. How about you, Percy. Fancy a bit of a jaunt?'

'I should like that very much,' the curate responded. 'Our … irregular arrival is the only time I've ever visited the town.'

'That's settled then,' Jago grinned. 'I shall ask Mrs Penna to serve breakfast a little earlier so we can leave before ten.'

Climbing to his feet, with the intention of seeking out the housekeeper, he gave a sidelong glance towards Charity before directing his next comment to her father. 'My appointment is at eleven and should last no more than an hour. Mayhap we can share a tankard of ale before lunch while Miss Shackleford visits one or two modistes.

Despite our provincial setting, I'm persuaded she will be impressed by the selection of fripperies on offer.'

'That sounds like an excellent idea,' the Reverend enthused, as always agreeable to giving the local ale a try. Jago nodded with a small smile and went in search of Mrs Penna.

'It sounds like an admirable plan,' Charity agreed. Then, determined to strike while Jago was no longer in the room, she added 'As you must have noticed, Father, I'm beginning to resemble that poor woman who sits outside the Red Lion at Blackmore.'

Naturally, her father had noticed nothing of the sort but as he looked over at her, his eyes suddenly widened. 'Tare an' hounds, Charity, when was the last time you actually changed that … rag you're wearing?'

'It's over a week, Father,' she responded sorrowfully, while inwardly thinking, *I'll give him a deuced rag*. Attempting sorrow through gritted teeth was not an easy task. The Reverend narrowed his eyes, and for a second, she wondered if she'd done it a bit too brown. After all, her father was much better at embellishing than she was. Jago would be back any minute, so she decided to help him along a bit.

'The fact of the matter is, Father, I am sore in need of a new dress.'

∞∞∞

By ten forty-five a.m. their carriage was approaching the outskirts of Falmouth. Charity had spent most of the journey in a light doze having slept poorly the night before. In truth, it was hardly surprising. Such a combination of elation and anxiety was never going to be conducive to a good night's sleep.

'I will meet you here in an hour,' Jago was saying as they alighted from the carriage. 'The main thoroughfare is that way.' He pointed towards a cobbled street snaking away from the harbour. 'I think you'll be pleasantly surprised.' This was directed to Charity, and she favoured him with a wide smile which wasn't missed by her eagle-eyed father.

'Am I to understand you're dangling after Mr Carlyon?' he commented bluntly as they carefully picked their way up the street, while Freddy sniffed happily at the interesting smells lingering on the cobbles.

'What a thing to say, Father!' Charity protested, her face flaming.

'Well, I'm not sure about setting your cap at someone who might well have more skeletons in his closet than an undertaker,' the Reverend sniffed.

Charity looked over at her father, alarmed at his vehemence, especially given that she was hoping Jago intended to ask for her hand in marriage in less than an hour's time.

'I believe Mr Carlyon to be an honourable man,' she commented carefully. 'I certainly do not believe him cognisant of the havey-cavey business his father may or may not be involved in.'

'I must concur with Miss Charity,' Percy interjected unexpectedly, earning him a sour look from the Reverend. 'Without Mr Carlyon's intervention, we might well even now be languishing at the bottom of Dartmouth harbour.'

'And consider, Father,' Charity went on, getting into her stride. 'If it's the thought of scandalising polite society that concerns you, our family have probably got more skeletons in the closet than the whole of the *ton* put together. Indeed, I'm persuaded we would be entirely ostracised if those overstuffed turkeys knew the half of it.'

The Reverend opened his mouth, then closed it again. The chit was right. He'd lost count of the number of times the Shackleford family had courted disaster, and in truth he did like Jago Carlyon. He and Charity would be a good match providing they could solve the problems of his murderous father, put the whole George Barnet thing to bed and the poor fellow could put up with her deuced sharp tongue.

Sighing, the Reverend sat down on a convenient bench while Charity perused a modiste's window. Absently stroking Freddy, he gave thought to their current situation. Truly, he was of the opinion that God was taking it all a bit far. Naturally, he hadn't expected to be handed eight perfect suitors on a plate, but he'd never imagined the Almighty might have such a partiality for drama. Mayhap he'd have a bit of a word when they got back to Blackmore.

∞∞∞

George Barnet leaned against the harbour wall and picked his teeth with the quill of a seagull feather. Since arriving the day before, he'd had no sleep and had lost count of the number of people he'd questioned about a Jago Cardell. To no avail. Angrily throwing the makeshift toothpick over the wall, George looked around the bustling quayside. In truth, he felt … uncomfortable, exposed. This wasn't his usual way of doing business at all. A few broken teeth in the early hours of the morning was generally all it took to get what he needed from most people.

He began to regret not bringing Will along with him. But his second-in-command needed to make sure they were ready for the next run, and in truth, George was … well … *embarrassed* as well as furious at the way Jago Cardell had hoodwinked him. If he didn't deal with the bastard soon, his reputation might never recover.

Shaking his head, the smuggler pushed himself off the wall and hesitated, unsure which way to go. In truth, he was bloody starving, and he remembered spying a pasty seller earlier. That and a tankard of ale would see him right. Once his attention was no longer on his stomach, he could decide what to do.

Deep in thought, he strode along the quayside towards the town. He hadn't yet tried asking in any of the taverns further away from the harbour. Generally, the less fortunate tended to stay in the rougher areas around the port. And beggars were more inclined to talk for the price of a husk of bread. But he realised he was going to need to cast his net wider.

Gritting his teeth, he waited for a carriage to go past, idly watching as it stopped a few yards along the street. Initially, he didn't register the dog as it jumped down the moment the coachman opened the door. But the next to descend was a clergyman. His heart suddenly thumping, George stepped back into the shadows and watched as the next passenger alighted.

It was her, the chit who'd unmasked him. He wanted to punch the air with glee. She turned back towards the coach to speak to another God botherer who was climbing down after her.

Then his heart slammed against his ribs as the last person finally alighted the coach. Initially unsure, as soon as the man lifted his head, George knew he'd found his quarry.

CHAPTER 23

'Well, my girl, if it's this fellow you want, I have no objection.' If her father's words were lacking in a little finesse, Charity didn't notice it. Indeed, she noticed very little except the smiling face of her newly intended as he rose to his feet and held out his hand.

With a bubbling laugh, she allowed him to seat her at the table. Percy, who'd appointed himself chief parcel carrier, was last to sit down after being divested of his veritable mountain of packages.

'I am delighted, Sir,' he enthused, leaning forward to shake Jago's hand.

'That's another one gone, Percy, only two more to go,' the Reverend commented jovially, having already partaken of two excellent tankards of ale.

'I've taken the liberty of ordering some Champagne,' Jago grinned to the curate. 'I hope you'll assist us in drinking it.'

'Indeed I will,' Percy beamed before turning to Charity. 'My dear, I am truly happy for you. I think you and Mr Carlyon are admirably suited and will deal very well together.'

'Thank you, Percy.' Charity's flushed face radiated happiness. 'Naturally, aside from Jago's father we will keep the news to ourselves until we've had a chance to share it with the rest of the family.'

'I will compose a letter this very evening,' the Reverend declared as the Champagne was brought to their table along with a generous portion of fresh bread and cheese.

'Well, this is likely to set you back a pretty penny,' Augustus Shackleford mused after they'd toasted the happy couple. 'Let's hope your father doesn't cut you off when he hears about the engagement.'

'Father!' Charity scolded, glancing anxiously up at Jago. To her surprise, he didn't show any anger at the Reverend's rudeness, only giving a rueful shake of his head.

'My father is much changed since I left two years ago,' Jago sighed. 'It's my fervent hope that news of my engagement will encourage him to begin living again.' He took Charity's hand and raised it to his lips, adding, 'But whatever my father's opinion, my happiness is my own to seek.' Charity felt her eyes fill with tears, and she gave a watery smile.

'It's just as well I've got plenty of other wealthy sons-in-law then,' the Reverend muttered with a sigh, holding out his glass for a refill.

An hour later, they were on their way back to Tredennick. Within minutes, Charity fell asleep with her head on his shoulder. Facing them, the Reverend and Percy were like two book ends, snoring in concert, with Freddy curled up happily between them.

Looking down at his new fiancée, Jago smiled, tucking her cloak around her. Fortunately, her parcels had fitted into the compartments underneath the seats. Evidently, her father had paid heed to her declaration that she needed a new dress. He fought the urge to laugh out loud. Charity was unaware that he'd been privy to the conversation.

Truly, he was looking forward to having many such sparring matches once they were wed.

After a while, inevitably, his thoughts turned to his father and the meeting he'd had with the solicitors earlier. Despite extensive enquires, old Mr Cuthbert had been unable to ascertain exactly what Morgan Carlyon had done with the three hundred pounds. The only thing he knew was the date the money had been taken from the bank. Two weeks before Genevieve's death.

Jago's inclination was to challenge his father about the money as soon as he got home but given that he was hoping to break the news of his intention to marry, any confrontation would have to wait. Wearily, Jago closed his eyes, just as the carriage lurched over a particularly deep pothole. Feeling his very bones rattle, his last thought before falling asleep was that Charity's parcels were clearly much heavier than they'd looked.

∞∞∞

Charity stared with satisfaction at herself in the mirror. The dress she'd chosen in Falmouth was a pale oyster which she fancied suited her colouring. In a rich satin brocade, it had a daringly low décolleté, and flared directly underneath her bosom. In the absence of any kind of lady's maid, Charity had simply tied her chestnut hair back using a matching ribbon as she was wont to do at home and draped the resulting wave over one shoulder. She and her twin were both fortunate enough to be in possession of natural curls that had long been the envy of their sisters, so the result was pleasing enough against the backdrop of her dress.

She had not seen Jago since their return from Falmouth and hoped that somehow he had persuaded his father to accept their engagement and mayhap even join them this evening. Then she thought back to the way the man had regarded her on the terrace and shivered.

Somehow she doubted Morgan Carlyon would welcome her with open arms.

Still, she squared her shoulders and picked up her shawl. If Jago's father thought to intimidate her into fleeing, he was in for a shock. Not one of her sisters had achieved wedded bliss without some kind of challenge, and if she was to follow in their footsteps, then so be it. The Master of Tredennick was about to discover that the Shackleford women were made of sterner stuff.

Draping the silky fabric over her shoulders, Charity caught sight of Stefan Petrock's letters still sitting forlornly on the small table. In light of what Jago had told them the evening before, it appeared the man couldn't bear to remain in Tredennick after the death of his love. Mayhap there were simply too many memories.

Picking up the bundle and placing them into her reticule, Charity resolved to return them to her father for disposal. Truly, she hoped the poor man had managed to find happiness elsewhere.

Snuffing out her candle and opening the door however, she suddenly reflected that they still had no explanation as to why Jago's father was shamming about his disability and why he'd spent so long searching for Stefan's letters.

Unless they hadn't been what he was looking for at all.

Determinedly, Charity put all thoughts of conspiracies from her mind. They would do well to focus on the imminent demise of George Barnet. Once his daughter's killer was behind bars, mayhap Morgan Carlyon would finally be able to truly put the past behind him and admit to his improved abilities.

Heading down the stairs, and crossing the entrance hall, she suddenly heard the sound of raised voices coming from the drawing room. Frowning, she paused. Almost certainly one of the voices belonged to Jago but she'd never heard the other man before. Her heart began to thud uncomfortably. There was only one person Jago would be arguing with.

Gritting her teeth, she marched determinedly towards the closed door, pausing only briefly to question whether she was being entirely totty-headed getting in between father and son. No, this was almost certainly about her. Squaring her shoulders, she lifted her head and pushed open the door.

Both men turned in surprise. This was the first time Charity had been in the same room as Jago's father, and the resemblance was even more striking than when she'd seen him on the stairs.

'Is this her?' he commented coldly.

'This is my wife-to-be, yes,' Jago responded, his voice equally wintery.

'This may come as a surprise to you gentlemen, but I actually have a name,' Charity snapped, shutting the door behind her.

There was a slight pause as Jago ran his hand across his brow. Then he sighed. 'Please forgive my deplorable manners, love,' he conceded with a bow. 'It is the first time my father has visited the drawing room since … in some time. He is clearly suffering the ill effects of too much exertion.' He turned to his stony-faced parent and continued, 'Father, allow me to introduce you to my fiancée, Miss Charity Shackleford.'

Morgan Carlyon stared impassively at her for several endless, uneasy moments.

'She's passably pretty,' he declared eventually, 'but you must know there is more to a marriage than a tempting armful.'

'Enough,' Jago ground out, his anger a palpable thing. 'If you find yourself unable to keep a civil tongue in your head, may I suggest you return to your bedchamber.'

Astonishingly, his father laughed, though there was no mirth in the sound. 'You think she will settle here, so far from her family?' he countered scathingly.

'I am standing directly in front of you,' Charity declared through gritted teeth, 'and I can assure you Mr Carlyon that I am perfectly capable of answering for myself.'

At that moment, the door opened behind them to admit her father and Percy. The look on the Reverend's face indicated he'd heard the altercation. Charity winced, closing her eyes, fully expecting him to give Jago's father a strong dressing down. But to her surprise, her father walked forward and gave a small bow.

'I am honoured to finally meet you, Sir,' he declared, his voice oozing sincerity. 'Allow me to introduce myself. Reverend Augustus Shackleford at your service. And this fellow behind me is my curate, Percy Noon. I see you have already met my daughter, Charity.' He gave a small chuckle. 'We also have a dog named Freddy who I'm entirely certain you will love once you get past the smell. Currently, he's enjoying a bowl of excellent mutton broth with Mrs Penna in the kitchen.'

Charity stared at her father open mouthed, wondering if he'd somehow been possessed.

Unfortunately, the Reverend hadn't finished. 'I must offer my deepest thanks for allowing us to stay,' he enthused, 'and I can tell that Jago has shared with you the happy news.' The clergyman held out his arms, a beatific smile on his face. 'It seems we are to become family.'

Morgan Carlyon looked as though he wished for nothing better than to shove the Reverend's words back down his blissful throat but could think of no way to do so.

'Would you like me to say a few words in thanks?' Reverend Shackleford continued into the resulting stony silence. 'I understand that sometimes such joyous news can be overwhelming.' He patted the seated man's hand before adding, 'As you're no doubt aware, Morgan – you don't object to me calling you Morgan do you? I mean we're almost family. Indeed, I would be *thrilled* if you'd call me Augustus – where was I? Oh, yes, as I'm sure you're aware ... *Morgan* ... our Lord really does move in the most mysterious ways. I mean, who would have thought a chance meeting in Dartmouth would result in two young people falling in love.'

By this point, Jago's father looked as though his desire to do violence had escalated to wringing the clergyman's neck. Indeed, his fingers gripping the armchair were almost white.

'What say you, Jago? Do you have any objection to me saying a few words?'

'As if I could stop you,' responded Jago drily, watching his future father-in-law with his eyebrows raised. 'Is this his normal behaviour?' the Cornishman murmured with a sidelong glance at Charity.

His bride to be shook her head. 'Did he perhaps drink too much at lunchtime, do you think, Percy?'

'*Our Father*,' yelled the Reverend abruptly, causing them all to jump.

'Are you entirely beef-witted?' Morgan Carlyon interrupted through gritted teeth. 'Get out of my house this instant and take your strumpet with you.'

'*Who art in Heaven*,' the Reverend continued even louder…

Incensed beyond all reason, the Master of Tredennick sprang to his feet and took two threatening steps forward. 'Desist, you imbecilic clergyman,' he roared, then abruptly stopped as he became aware that Reverend Shackleford had fallen silent and everyone in the room was staring.

'I wasn't aware you'd regained the use of your legs, Father,' Jago commented, his voice deceptively mild.

'A true miracle,' the Reverend murmured with a surreptitious wink at Charity.

Morgan Carlyon stared for a second at the expressionless face of his son before hurriedly collapsing back into his chair. 'The extreme emotion must have caused my legs to momentarily work,' he retaliated with a forced groan. 'Clearly, it was the anger at these ... *interlopers*,' he continued, glaring at Reverend Shackleford's serene countenance.

'How long have you been able to walk?' Jago asked steadily, evidently unimpressed with his father's explanation.

'Certainly since we arrived,' the Reverend commented.

Jago shook his head. 'Why? What did you hope to gain? You must know I wanted nothing more than for you to regain the use of your legs.' He paused, but his father remained coldly silent. 'I believed that finding Genevieve's killer would finally allow you to put the past to bed.' Jago sighed at length.

'And yet you bring these ... persons into my house, forever reminding me of the daughter I lost.'

'Charity was the one who discovered Jack's real identity,' Jago erupted. 'And she risked her life in doing so. It's she you must thank when you watch the bastard swing.'

'Well, this has been most enlightening, but I think I've heard quite enough.' An unknown voice came from the shadows, and Charity drew a terrified breath as the subject of their conversation stepped out from behind the draught screen in the window, a pistol in each hand.

'Who the hell are you?' Morgan Carlyon ground out, seeming not to have noticed the weapons pointing directly at them.

'I'm the bastard you're apparently hoping to watch swing,' George Barnet answered calmly.

'How did you find us?' Jago questioned, ruthlessly compressing the sick dread that threatened to swamp him.

'Ah, Mr Cardell,' Barnet declared expansively, 'who, it turns out was not Mr *Cardell* at all. You'd think I, of all people would have guessed.'

He gave a small chuckle and shook his head. 'I have to say the trunk at the back of your carriage needs some padding.' He turned his attention to Charity.

'So this is the bitch who found me out. Was it at the Castle?' Feeling the very same terror that had gripped her the first time she had seen this man, Charity stared at him mutely.

'What, no thanks for introducing you to your husband-to-be?' the gang leader taunted. 'Shame your engagement is going to be so short lived, though I don't think everyone here will be entirely sorry.' He looked with curiosity at Morgan Carlyon. 'So what's wrong with your legs old man?'

'He suffered an apoplexy after you murdered his daughter,' Jago burst out, his rage getting the better of him.

'So *that's* why you came to Dartmouth,' George declared. 'And here's me just thinking you were just after the reward.' He shrugged. 'So, what was her name, this daughter of yours?' He addressed the question to Jago's father.

'Genevieve Carlyon,' Jago spat in answer. 'She was travelling home on the *Endeavour.*

Abruptly, George Barnet swung the pistol towards Jago, saying in quiet fury, 'Speak again, and I'll shoot off your trinkets.' Then he turned back to Morgan Carlyon, regarding the pale, sweating man with interest. 'She was one of the passengers pushed off the cliff?' He cocked his head at the barely perceptible nod he received in return. Then he grinned.

'Well, I hate to break it to you, Mr Carlyon, but you've got the wrong man. How ironic is that?' This time he laughed and shook his head. 'Whoever scuttled the *Endeavour* and sent her passengers over that bloody cliff, it wasn't me.'

CHAPTER 24

After leaving his horse in the care of the stable hand, Richard Tregear strode towards the entrance to Tredennick House. He'd been unavoidably delayed at the mine, and by the time he was able to leave, the last of the daylight had fled, making it too dangerous to push his mount in the dark. Climbing the steps to the entrance, he hesitated before pulling the doorbell. Mrs Penna would undoubtedly be busy supervising the final preparations to the engagement dinner. He did not need to drag her away. If this door was locked, he'd make his way round to the kitchens. He gave the door knob an experimental twist, and to his relief found it unlocked.

Stepping out of the cold, he sighed with relief and shrugged off his coat, hanging it in the small alcove provided for such a purpose. Hearing the murmur of voices, he made his way towards the drawing room, thankful they'd apparently not yet gone into dinner. He was just about to push open the door, an apology on his lips when all of a sudden he heard Jago's voice raised in anger. His heart sank, thinking his friend's ire directed towards the Master of Tredennick.

Then came a male voice he didn't recognise. He couldn't quite hear what was said, but the threat was unmistakable. Richard stepped back from the door quietly, carefully, and weighed his options. Clearly, he needed to fetch help. Where were the bloody footmen? Taking another step backwards, the estate manager thought for a second, then hurried towards the kitchens.

∞∞∞

'*Liar!*' Jago's father spat just the one word, his body trembling with rage.

'Why would I lie?' retorted Barnet evenly. 'Believe me I've done much, much worse than throw someone off a bloody cliff.' He gave a wide smile. 'All this time you've been barking up the wrong tree.'

He turned to Jago. 'Did daddy send you?' he taunted. 'Off you trotted like a good little hero, thinking to feed me a bag of bloody moonshine. But the thing is, you're not that good at shamming it. Not like your father here. Now there's a man I could grow to like.'

'What the devil are you talking about?' Jago said through gritted teeth.

'I've often wondered who carried out that job,' George mused. 'I mean not many free traders would risk offending me by attempting a run on my patch. But nobody would admit to it. And then, no one seemed to know who'd stumped up the blunt, or why - especially given the *Endeavour's* hold was empty and any smuggler worth his salt would have found that out easily.' He cocked his head on one side. 'Who did you want dead?' he asked, grinning as the seated man flinched. 'You didn't know your daughter was on that ship, did you?'

He winked at Jago who was staring at his father in horror. 'The three hundred pounds,' he breathed.

'Got the job done cheap. They must have been purse-pinched,' Barnet chuckled, then shook his head. 'Well, as delightful as this little heart-to-heart has been, I think it's time I was on my way. Not sure who I should kill first though.' He frowned, pretending to think.

'You only have four bullets, but there are five of us,' blurted Percy suddenly.

'Ah, it speaks,' George commented jovially. 'And since you so very kindly reminded me, mayhap I'll save you until last.' He waved the pistol in his left hand before winking lewdly at Charity who hadn't moved, her terror absolute. 'Thought I'd take you with me, sweetheart. We can have us some fun before I wring your pretty little neck.'

'I have money. Take it,' Jago grated desperately. 'The Customs men know who you are, Barnet. It's only a matter of time before they catch up with you. You can use the coin to buy passage to the Americas.'

'I've got plenty of blunt and more places to hide out that you could ever imagine,' the smuggler scoffed. 'The bloody Gobblers won't catch me.' Then he stretched out his hand and pointed the pistol at Jago.

There was the deafening sound of a gunshot just as Charity broke free of her paralysis and screamed, 'No!' knocking the smuggler's arm upwards. Jago acted immediately, throwing himself at Barnet and knocking the two of them backwards.

'Thunder an' turf,' Reverend Shackleford muttered as he hurried to retrieve one of the pistols that had fallen to the floor. The other was trapped between the two grappling men. Hastily, the Reverend sniffed the barrel of the one in his hand. No smell of gunpowder.

'His pistol's dead,' the clergyman shouted to Jago, just as Barnet managed to get his pistol hand free. Registering the Reverend's shout, the smuggler lifted his arm and slammed the barrel of the gun down onto Jago's forehead.

Dazed, Jago couldn't stop his opponent from tipping him onto his back where Barnet lifted his hand again to hit him with the weapon a second time.

Trembling, the Reverend pointed the gun in his hand. 'Dear God, please let me do it,' he whispered. Suddenly, the weapon was snatched out of his hand, and incredulously, he watched as Morgan Carlyon pointed the pistol at Barnet's exposed back and fired.

There was a sudden shocked silence as the gang leader slumped down onto Jago, then the drawing room door was flung open as Richard Tregear charged in, followed closely by two footmen and Freddy.

∞∞∞

'I'm sorry Father, but whatever God says, I cannot feel anything other than relief at his death,' Charity declared with a shudder.

'I doubt any of us are going to lose any sleep over the varmint's demise,' snorted the Reverend. 'If ever there was a prime candidate for the tea and brimstone club, it was George Barnet.' He shrugged and took a sip of his brandy. 'Saved the Revenue men a job if you ask me.' He paused and sighed. 'Now Morgan Carlyon? Well, that's an entirely different matter.'

Charity's eyes followed her father's troubled glance to the door where Jago, Morgan and Richard had disappeared after seeing to the removal of the smuggler's body.

They'd been gone nearly an hour after Jago had briefly returned to inform them that Mrs Penna would be providing some refreshment.

'I will send word to Philip Lander first thing in the morning,' he murmured, squeezing her hand. 'It's all over love, you have nothing more to fear.' Heedless of the presence of her father and Percy, Charity jumped up with a small sob and pressed herself into his arms. Closing his eyes, Jago held her tight for a second, then firmly put her from him. 'I have to speak with my father,' he whispered, willing her to understand.

Charity had simply nodded and watched him leave.

Since then, there had been no word, and despite having had no dinner, not even Percy felt inclined to eat the cold repast Mrs Penna brought in half an hour later. The housekeeper had been understandably subdued, not to mention entirely confused as to why a dead body had suddenly turned up in their drawing room.

'Where have they put him, do you know?' Charity had to ask.

'It's my belief he's in the wood store,' Mrs Penna shuddered. Then seeing Charity's white face, and shaking hands, she added, 'I'll fetch you some warm milk, my dear. A little bit of brandy in it will put an end to your shivers.'

In truth, the milk and brandy had helped, but when another forty-five minutes had passed, Charity could stand it no longer. 'Freddy needs to do his business,' she declared. 'I'll fetch my cloak.'

Crossing the entrance hall to the stairs, Charity stared anxiously at the closed door of the small sitting room. If George Barnet had been speaking the truth, what possible reason could Jago's father have had to deliberately wreck a ship? Shaking her head, she hurried upstairs to her bedchamber and shrugged on Genevieve's cloak.

Five minutes later, she breathed a sigh of relief as she stepped outside into the cold invigorating air. Unclipping Freddy's lead, Charity gave the foxhound the opportunity to stretch his legs and free her hands to take advantage of the cloak's wonderfully deep fur-lined pockets. Drawing the hood over her head, Charity tucked her hands down as far as they would go, hunching down into the soft fur around the neck.

Abruptly, her fingers touched the edge of something wedged deep inside the folds of the pocket. It felt like some kind of parchment. Pinching it between her forefinger and thumb, she finally managed to draw out a small square of folded paper. Frowning, she pulled her other hand free of its pocket and moving towards the candlelight flickering in the drawing room window, she started to open it.

∞∞∞

Despite his anger, Jago regarded his father's waxy features with concern. They were seated in Genevieve's sitting room. There was no fire in the grate, and the room felt cold and stale. But despite the temperature, Morgan Carlyon was sweating profusely.

Swearing softly, Jago got to his feet and poured three large brandies. 'Do you wish me to leave?' Richard asked Jago, accepting the glass.

Jago shook his head as he handed another glass to his father. 'We are beyond that now,' he sighed sitting back down. 'There will be no more secrets, and I will need you as a witness.'

The Master of Tredennick seemed hardly aware of the conversation as he swallowed the brandy in one gulp and held the empty glass in shaking hands.

Leaning wearily back against his chair, Jago took a sip of his own brandy, staring over the rim at his father's white face. 'Why?' he asked simply at length.

For a second, he thought his father wasn't going to answer, then raising haunted eyes, he muttered, 'Johnson knew.'

'You mean *Endeavour's* captain?' Jago queried, struggling to contain his impatience. 'What did he know?'

'He knew I was financing the Helford free traders.'

'You were what?' Jago bit out, the horror in his voice unfeigned.

'I thought the mine was finished,' his father shouted, showing more animation than he had since entering the room. 'Others are failing, all over Cornwall. Why should Wheal Tredennick be any different? I did it for you.'

'Don't you dare,' Jago shot back savagely, jumping to his feet and pointing an unsteady finger towards his father who blanched and leaned back. 'Don't you *dare* use me as an excuse, you self-centred bastard.' His voice turned icy as he added, 'You always hated the mine.

You couldn't wait to hand the reins over to me. You had no bloody idea whether it was making a profit or not.'

Richard stood up, inserting himself between the two men and placed a calming hand on his friend's heaving shoulder. 'You need to hear him out, Jago,' he advised softly.

Tossing back the rest of his brandy, Jago threw himself back in his seat, relishing the burn of the fiery liquid as it slid down his throat.

'I didn't know he was bringing Genevieve home,' his father whispered brokenly.

'Who did it? Who did you pay to murder over fifty innocent people?'

Morgan shook his head. 'Stefan took care of it.'

'Stefan Petrock?' Jago shook his head. 'What the devil did he have to do with it?'

'I was paying him,' his father answered, his voice becoming stronger. 'He knew the score. Knew that it wouldn't be me who paid the price of discovery.'

'What happened to him?' Jago asked, feeling suddenly sick.

The Master of Tredennick abruptly started laughing. 'He's in a trunk in my room,' he finally managed to gasp, tears of mirth streaming down his face. 'The one with my chamber pot on it.'

Jago grimaced in horror at the knowledge his father had been sharing his bedchamber with a corpse for nearly two years. He looked over at Richard whose face clearly revealed the same shock.

Jago had no idea what to say. He simply watched as the tears of mirth streaming down his father's face became tears of anguish, and he finally realised that something inside the Master of Tredennick had been irreparably broken.

∞∞∞

Despite the light from the window, Charity was unable to see clearly what was on the parchment. Frowning, she held it up closer and finally managed to distinguish the signature. It was Stefan Petrock.

Heart thudding, Charity called Freddy and hurried back inside, faltering briefly at the sound of raised voices coming from the small sitting room. Then, shaking her head, she continued on into the drawing room where her father and Percy had finally succumbed to the lure of ham and pickles.

'I think I may have found something,' she commented breathlessly, brandishing the paper.

Picking up one of the candles, she positioned it next to her chair. After a few seconds she looked up. 'It's a confession.'

∞∞∞

Morgan Carlyon did not survive the night. Jago had not been surprised.

They'd removed the trunk containing Stefan Petrock's body, but Morgan had showed no emotion. He'd simply allowed himself to be put to bed like a child. The next morning he was gone.

To Jago's astonishment, Charity, her father and Percy had been able to fill in the missing pieces of the story, and the sympathy in Charity's eyes as she handed him Stefan's letters and confession made him want to howl.

Morgan Carlyon had used Stefan's love for Genevieve to persuade the young man to go along with his schemes, declaring the coin made from their illegal activities would provide Genevieve with the lifestyle she'd been accustomed to and promising their union would receive his blessing on her return.

At first, things went according to plan, but their luck ran out as Captain Johnson of the *Endeavour* discovered who was behind the spate of runs on goods arriving in Falmouth from the far east. As a long-standing friend, Johnson had given Morgan the benefit of the doubt when he'd claimed to know nothing, blaming the whole scheme on Stefan. But it was only a matter of time before he discovered the truth.

Morgan Carlyon blackmailed his daughter's lover into getting rid of the threat. Unfortunately, neither had suspected that their smuggler associates would not stop with the death of one man when they had the chance to remove all witnesses.

Neither did they know that Genevieve would be one of them.

According to Stefan, terrified that Jago would begin to suspect, Morgan blamed the murders on the infamous Jack and encouraged his son on a wild goose chase. But clearly, he'd reckoned without Stefan's conscience.

They would never know exactly how Stefan died. The body was too far decayed to tell. Indeed, all they really knew for certain was that Morgan Carlyon suffered the apoplexy almost immediately after, confining him to his bed, at least for a few months.

Did he hide the fact that he'd regained the use of his legs to give him an alibi should Stefan's body ever be discovered?

Had Stefan admitted to writing a confession before breathing his last? Was that what Morgan had been looking for?

It seemed certain that Stefan had written his admission of guilt down on paper as a last resort. But whether it was from fear or remorse, only a dead man could tell them.

CHAPTER 25

GEORGE BARNET's body was hung in gruesome fashion on the harbour wall at Falmouth as a warning to other free traders, though whether it had the intended effect was debatable, especially as by the middle of April, Napoleon had indeed abdicated, and the war in Europe was finally over, making goods from France even more readily available.

Nevertheless, his demise meant that the Reverend, Percy and Charity were finally free to return home.

They had been in Tredennick barely a week, but to Charity it felt like almost a lifetime. So much had changed since they'd left Blackmore less than a sennight ago.

Indeed, sitting in the new Master of Tredennick's carriage, she felt as though she was leaving part of herself behind, and though she looked forward to seeing Blackmore and her family again, she already knew that her heart belonged in Cornwall with the man she had so unexpectedly fallen in love with.

Heedless of onlookers, Jago had held her to him as though he could not bear to let her go, and even as she revelled in the strength of his arms, Charity realised he was actually afraid. Afraid that once she was home, she would not wish to return. That in letting her go, he was losing her forever.

Leaning back to look up at him, Charity touched his cheek with her fingers and smiled through her tears. 'A mere three months,' she whispered. 'It will pass in the blink of an eye.'

'It will feel like a lifetime.' She almost laughed at his frustrated whisper and shook her head.

'You have much to do, Mr Carlyon if you wish to ready our home for my return. Once I'm your wife, you will undoubtedly have other things on your mind.' She watched the gold in his eyes darken at her hint and chuckled.

'This will be the first and last time you leave me,' Jago growled, bending his head for one last kiss. Charity simply nodded and smiled.

'I love you, Jago Carlyon,' she murmured.

His answer was to kiss her again, suddenly desperate to keep her with him at any cost.

'Well, much as I don't wish to put a rub in the way of true love,' her father commented sourly from inside the coach, 'but at this rate, I'm going to need the privy again before we get to the bottom of the deuced drive.'

It was two full days before the carriage finally pulled up outside the vicarage, and Charity watched eagerly for her twin as the coach driver carefully negotiated the narrow lane from the village. However, it seemed Chastity was not yet returned from Torquay, and it was Prudence who came out to greet them.

After giving her sister a brief, fierce hug, the youngest Shackleford sister had said a fervent, 'Thank God you're back. If I have to reassure stepmother that her headache is *not* Dengue fever one more time, I swear I shall scream...' Then she paused, leaned back and looked at Charity narrowly, before adding, 'Not that I ever doubted you possessed hidden talents dearest sister, but how the devil did you manage to seduce a man in *Salcombe?*'

It was another three days before Grace arrived home with Chastity, and it seemed their holiday had been largely uneventful. After announcing vehemently that she was not yet ready to become a mother, Chastity declared she was beyond glad to get home for a rest. 'You wouldn't believe how loud a baby can cry,' she confided. 'For a tiny scrap of a thing, Henrietta's wails could be heard down the street. She's undoubtedly taking after Hope.'

If she'd been surprised at the enthusiastic hug her twin gave her as soon as she walked through the door, Chastity didn't show it, but merely tucked her arm inside her twin's and commiserated, 'Was it so terrible being stuck with Father and Percy for more than two whole weeks?'

Unsurprisingly, the news of Charity's unexpected engagement prompted a complete change of plan. Instead of gathering up in London, the entire family would now congregate at Blackmore for the wedding.

Of course, the groom would have to undergo thorough inquiry from all five Shackleford husbands beforehand in order to confirm that he was every bit as dicked in the nob as the rest of them...

And now, as spring gave way to summer, it was two months, three weeks and four days since Charity had left Tredennick. Not that she'd been counting the days or anything.

Watching Jago's carriage approach the imposing front entrance to Blackmore, Charity felt her nerves stretch to breaking point. While she was grateful the entire family hadn't congregated on the steps, the stern face of Nicholas Sinclair was more than enough to send any prospective groom with less bottle running for the hills. Her father and Percy were there too, as was Grace and, of course, Chastity.

For once, she was entirely glad of her twin's unbridled enthusiasm. Indeed, it was Chastity who pushed her towards the steps as the carriage finally came to a stop.

Unaccountably shy, Charity watched as Jago unfolded his big frame from the carriage, but his lazy grin as he caught sight of her promptly put an end to her nerves, and the opening of his arms was all the encouragement she needed to throw herself into them.

At the top of the steps, the Duke of Blackmore remarked drily that as first impressions went, Jago Carlyon appeared to be woefully short of good manners and would almost certainly fail to measure up to polite society's standards of behaviour.

So, all in all, he would undoubtedly fit into the family perfectly.

∞∞∞

The wedding took place three weeks later. As ever, it was enjoyed by all the residents of Blackmore, though the villagers agreed that this one wasn't nearly as grand as the last two attended by 'er Royalness.

There were also slight concerns that Miss Charity had chosen a heathen Cornishman over a solid Devonshire lad, but most agreed that the groom had so far exhibited none of the wildness associated with *them over the border.*

Of course, the general consensus was that there was undoubtedly a smoky tale behind the happy couple's courtship, but it was unanimously agreed that they should put it from their minds and simply enjoy the festivities. After all, it was only a matter of time before Reverend Shackleford downed a few too many tankards of ale down at the Red Lion and they found out what it was.

THE END

The Reverend and the rest of the Shackleford family return in Chastity: Book Seven of The Shackleford Sisters, now available from Amazon

KEEPING IN TOUCH

Thank you so much for reading *Charity,* I really hope you enjoyed it. For any of you who'd like to connect, I'd really love to hear from you. Feel free to contact me via my facebook page:
https://www.facebook.com/beverleywattsromanticcomedyauthor
or my website:
http://www.beverleywatts.com
If you'd like me to let you know as soon as my next book is available, sign up to my newsletter by copying and pasting the link below into your browser and I'll keep you updated about that and all my latest releases.

https://motivated-teacher-3299.ck.page/143a008c18

And lastly, thanks a million for taking the time to read this story. If you'd like a sneak peek at *Chastity:* Book 7 of The Shackleford Sisters, turn the page...

CHASTITY

In the eyes of her family, Chastity Shackleford was impulsive, flighty, overly emotional and inclined to sentimental overtures. All in all, a disaster waiting to happen should she accept the Duke of Blackmore's offer of a Season in London. But what else was she to do since her twin sister and best friend had abandoned her for the wilds of Cornwall?

Naturally she might have hoped that disaster had waited a little longer before striking, but at least she faced the possibility of marriage with someone who had all his own teeth. The fact that the gentleman was also wanted for murder was a little off-putting, but then one couldn't have everything.

When Christian Stanhope was forced to jump ship after being accused of a crime he didn't commit, he'd never expected to return to England. But then he'd never expected to become the next Earl of Cottesmore either.

However, if he was to survive the merciless world of England's aristocracy, clearing his name was essential. And for that he needed the help of his former First Lieutenant Nicholas Sinclair, now the Duke of Blackmore. But first he had to convince the Duke that he was not guilty of a heinous murder committed seventeen years earlier. A task easier said than done.

But, just when he despaired of ever finding the real culprit and bringing him to justice, help, or possibly hindrance, arrived from an unexpected quarter...

PROLOGUE

Chastity Shackleford's twin sister had accused her of being an incurable romantic. Indeed, she herself would have agreed entirely, three weeks, four days and seven hours ago, even if she was of the opinion that Charity's words had been a trifle blunt.

But, three weeks, four days and seven hours was precisely the length of time it had taken to finally knock the last vestige of romance from her soul.

And now, shivering alone in the Earl of Cottesmore's vast, cold bed, she couldn't help but reflect - mostly in disbelief, it had to be said - at the unfortunate incident that had occasioned her current unhappy position.

In truth, it could be argued that her present dilemma should be laid firmly at the door of her twin, given that it was Charity who had suggested she accept the Duke of Blackmore's offer of a Season in London.

Truly, having shared a womb, and spending practically every waking moment together since then, one would have thought Charity possessed enough common sense to realise that allowing her twin to brave the marriage mart on her own was quite simply a recipe for disaster.

Indeed, Chastity was persuaded she would not now be in this most vexing position had Charity herself not fallen unexpectedly in love and abandoned Blackmore for the wilds of Cornwall with her new husband.

Gritting her teeth to stop them chattering, Chastity turned her head and eyed the barely visible door apprehensively. She didn't know which would be worse. The Earl of Cottesmore actually noticing her in his bed before climbing into it or discovering her presence once he was between the sheets. Definitely the latter. She sincerely hoped he was not in the habit of taking a pistol to bed.

Of course, what she should be doing was considering not how the Earl might effect her demise - or indeed what the devil he would do with her body once he'd done the effecting–but what words she could best use to persuade him that murdering her in his bed was actually *not* going to help with their current predicament. Or rather *her* current predicament. Although, to be fair, he wasn't yet *aware* of *her* current predicament.

He was a man of the world. Surely he would listen while she explained the reason for her unexpected presence in his bed. Naturally, she'd have to convince him that she wasn't there to trap him into marriage. Well, she *was*, but it was purely business. He needed to know that she'd entirely eschewed affairs of the heart, though, in all honesty, there was nothing romantic about freezing to death in a lord's bed. Which, if he didn't get a move on, was a very real possibility. But then, mayhap she'd be simply saving him the job. What on earth had possessed her that she could *ever* have believed this to be a good idea? To be hon…

Her thoughts screeched to a halt as she heard a sudden noise outside the window…

CHAPTER 1

Two weeks earlier..

The ball held at the Duke and Duchess of Blackmore's London townhouse to herald in the year of 1815 was widely regarded as the most prestigious event of the year. Whilst the lingering euphoria of Napoleon's exile to the Isle of Elba undoubtedly contributed to the festive atmosphere, the ball's success was in no small part due to the popularity and standing within the *ton* of Nicholas Sinclair and his beautiful, though unconventional, wife, Grace.

The fact that the Duchess was the daughter of a local vicar appeared to have been forgotten or, if not forgotten, certainly disregarded. Indeed, it was widely agreed that her grace was looking simply radiant, as were those of her equally unconventional sisters who were present.

And if many of the gentlemen attending sported anxious frowns concerning the economic plight of Great Britain in the aftermath of the twenty-three-year war in Europe, well, such cares and considerations were easily drowned in a few glasses of the Duke's most excellent port.

It had to be said that whilst the Duchess of Blackmore's humble origins were generally overlooked, the presence of her father at events such as these, or rather his penchant for generating unfortunate incidents such as the one involving Queen Charlotte and the duck pond, was naturally of some concern to the rest of the family.

However, exile to the small, delightful drawing room along with Malcolm, the Duke's long-standing and similarly outspoken valet, was in no way seen as a slight by the Reverend. In truth, Augustus Shackleford shouldn't really have been in London at all and was entirely delighted to be foregoing the tedious and stultifying conversation enjoyed by polite society. Especially as the table was positively groaning under the weight of a delicious array of the cook's tempting tarts and pastries, and the jug of port sitting tantalisingly on the sideboard was entirely up to his son-in-law's usual standards.

Naturally, Percy Noon, the Reverend's long-suffering curate was also present, as were the two younger Shacklefords, Prudence and Anthony. Both, much to their older sisters' relief, had absolutely no desire to take part in the festivities. Indeed, Prudence had declared that she'd rather have her toenails removed with red hot pincers.

And then of course there was the Reverend's foxhound Freddy who was perfectly content lying under the table ready to demolish any crumbs that happened to fall his way.

All three men were in a particularly jocular mood as the clock approached midnight, and Reverend Shackleford was persuaded that this was possibly the best New Year's Eve he'd ever spent. For one thing, he hadn't seen Agnes, his wife, since well before supper and was confident she would be happily discussing with all the other tabbies her latest obsession with yellow fever for hours yet.

His only daughter of marriageable age as yet unwed was Chastity, and he wasn't about to do anything that might throw a rub in the way of Grace's plans to bring the chit out.

So all in all, he was happy to make himself scarce until he was required to give his blessing to whoever was unfortunate enough to land himself with the totty-headed baggage.

* * *

THE TOTTY-HEADED baggage in question was currently being escorted onto the dance floor by Viscount Trebworthy. Indeed, her father would have been ecstatic considering the young man was heir to a dukedom and rich as Croesus to boot. Unfortunately, he was also tall and skinny with breath like an open privy. In truth, Chastity was not entirely convinced she was actually going to survive the Cotillion. Determinedly, she fixed her gaze on his bony chest and endeavoured to breathe through her mouth. Hopefully, he would think her completely devoid of any personality and seek to be rid of her as soon as they vacated the dance floor.

Regrettably that proved not to be the case, and in desperation, pleading a sudden excessive thirst, Chastity sent the Viscount off in search of a glass of water, then promptly made herself scarce. Finally collapsing onto a chair hidden in a quiet corner.

Dear Lord, but she missed her twin. Charity was the only sister who'd been unable to join the family for Christmas. The distance and the state of the roads between Falmouth and London made travelling such a distance nigh on impossible during the cold, wet winter months. Why the devil did Charity have to go and choose a man from deuced *Cornwall*? Notwithstanding the small detail that Jago Carlyon was perfect for her twin, surely she could have settled on someone equally perfect who didn't live so bloody *far away*.

Sighing, Chastity furtively watched the room from her secluded corner. According to her dance card, her next two dances were unclaimed. So it was imperative she keep her head down for the rest of the Reel and more importantly the Waltz that was to follow. The thought of being in such *close* proximity to the Viscount for a whole ten minutes was too desperate to even contemplate.

It had to be said, that so far, London was not living up to her romantic notions. In actual fact, it was failing dismally. She was reminded at every turn why exactly she and Charity had hated it so much growing up. Reading her stepmother's periodicals and gossip sheets from the security of Blackmore was one thing. Actually mixing with polite society was another matter entirely.

She'd been in London for nearly three weeks and already she realised that most members of the *ton* were vain, self-centred peacocks baring no resemblance to her girlish imaginings.

Coming back to the present, Chastity suddenly realised that the reel had finished, and guests were busy regrouping for the waltz. To her horror, she spied Viscount Trebworthy heading determinedly her way. Damn and blast, she'd been rumbled. Wildly, she glanced about, abruptly taking note of a tall, dark-haired gentleman leaning nonchalantly against the wall to her left. He was alone and sipping on a glass of punch. From her angle, she was unable to see his face, but truthfully, as long as his breath didn't smell like the bottom of a cesspool, she could survive facing him for ten minutes.

But she only had mere seconds to convince the stranger to dance with her. Without giving herself any time to reconsider, Chastity jumped to her feet and tapped the man on his shoulder. As soon as he turned his head and directed his icy-blue eyes towards her, she entirely lost the use of her tongue. Dear God, the man was an Adonis. Albeit one with raven black hair.

Far, far too late, she wondered what a man of such exceptional looks was doing propping up a wall at the back of a ballroom. Alone. His expression gave her an immediate answer. It was one of disdainful boredom, but his eyes, oh his eyes. They were the colour of winter. And so cold that she took an involuntary step back. What the devil had she been thinking, attracting the attention of such a mysterious individual.

Out of the corner of her eye, she saw Viscount Trebworthy stumble to a stop. For a second, he remained still, then he turned and almost ran in the opposite direction. *Deuced coward*, she thought, ignoring the fact that less than thirty seconds ago she'd have been thanking the Almighty for such a reprieve.

'May I help you?' She became aware that the Adonis was speaking. And more than that. His incredible eyes were regarding her as if she were something nasty he'd found on the bottom of his shiny Hessian boot.

Which made her next words all the more preposterous. Indeed, she could scarce believe the sound of her own voice as she uttered them. 'I was wondering if you were engaged for this dance, sir.'

His expression turned incredulous.

'Am to understand you are propositioning me Madam?' His voice was deep, husky and quite possibly the most arresting sound she'd ever heard. Her face coloured up as she stammered, 'I am uncertain as to what exactly a proposition would entail, sir. I am merely asking to take up ten minutes of your time.'

Charity was aware they were beginning to attract speculative glances and was entirely certain that if he didn't hold out his arm soon, she would die of mortification. What the deuce had she been thinking? She would never live this down. *Never*. If anybody had actually *heard* her request, she was ruined. Underneath her pale lilac dress, the sweat trickled down her back.

Her relief was short lived when a second later, he gave a lazy grin and held out his hand. If his voice had been arresting, his smile was quite simply devastating. Her heart slammed against her chest, and the voice inside her head was screaming *run*. After casting a wild glance round at the interested stares being cast their way, Chastity knew she had no choice but to brave it out. Truly, her idiocy was breathtaking.

Biting her lip, she bent her head in acknowledgement and laying her hand over his, she allowed him to lead her to the floor. At first, he did not speak but simply swept her into his arms as the first strains of the waltz began to play. Her relief that he was an accomplished dancer was almost hysterical. *Ten minutes*, she just had to get through the next ten minutes. It was nothing. She stared determinedly at his chest as they whirled round the dance floor. So insistent was the mantra in her head, she hadn't realised that she'd actually spoken the words aloud.

'If this is not to your liking, my lady, I am more than happy to forgo the rest of the dance.' Alarmed, she looked up, terrified she'd offended him, and he was about to leave her standing alone on the dance floor.

'I… I… Please accept my apologies, Sir,' she faltered. 'I am aware that my conduct has so far been less than exemplary. I don't… That is… I'm not usually in the habit of asking strangers to dance with me.'

'I'm very glad to hear it,' was his dry response. 'I take it you were seeking to escape Viscount Trebworthy.'

'Oh no, not at all,' she lied desperately.

To her surprise, he chuckled. 'I have had occasion to be within breathing distance of the individual, and you have my complete sympathy. The man is desperately in need of a good dentist.'

Reassured that he appeared to have a human side after all, Chastity gave a timorous smile. 'Do you have a name, sir?' she asked hesitantly when it appeared he'd said all he intended to. If any of her family had happened to spy her on the dance floor, they would at least expect her to know the gentleman's name. And she had little doubt that she was being observed by at least one of her sisters. 'My name is…' she continued, only to pause, fearing she was committing another faux pas in offering it.

'Miss Chastity Shackleford,' he finished. Surprised he knew her name, she was unsure what to say. For some bizarre reason, his admission made her braver, and her stare was almost challenging as she waited for him to offer his own. Instead, he gazed down at her impassively for several endless uneasy moments and she felt her bravado slip away. Somehow, in asking his name, she had stepped over some imaginary line. His beautiful eyes were guarded, but they had a slight mocking gleam that had her desperately wanting to know who he was and why he would look at her with such disdain. She did not think it due to her earlier boldness.

Despite her confusion, Chastity was almost sorry as the music finally drew to a close. 'Thank you for the rescue,' she murmured to his chest as she prepared to step out of his arms. 'It was most kind of you to take pity on me, Sir.' He gave a short laugh, and the bitterness in it had her looking up at him in surprise. She became aware that he had not released her from his grip and felt the first stirrings of alarm.

'I've been called many things, Miss Shackleford,' he commented drily, 'but to my knowledge, never kind.' To Chastity's relief, he finally loosed her hands and stepped back slightly. She took hold of her skirts in preparation for her customary curtsy.

'However, if you choose to consider my actions so,' he continued, causing her to pause and look back up at him in unease, 'then perhaps I can impose upon you to do a small kindness for me in return.' He stared down at her with the same mocking gleam in his eyes, and Chastity immediately felt the last of her boldness disappear.

'Naturally, I am happy to be of assistance if I can,' she murmured, the uncertainty in her voice a direct contrast to her polite words.

His smile became almost feral at her obvious discomfort. 'Then perhaps you would be so kind as to inform Nicholas Sinclair that Christian Stanhope has returned and will await his pleasure.'

And with that, he gave a low, perfectly executed bow and walked away.

Chastity is now available from Amazon

Turn the page for a full list of all my books currently available on Amazon

ALSO BY BEVERLEY WATTS ON AMAZON

The Shackleford Sisters
Book 1 - Grace
Book 2 - Temperance
Book 3 - Faith
Book 4 - Hope
Book 5 - Patience
Book 6 - Charity
Book 7 - Chastity
Book 8 - Prudence
Book 9 - Anthony

The Shackleford Legacies
Book 1 - Jennifer
Book 2 - Mercedes
Book 3 - Roseanna will be released on March 27th 2025

The Shackleford Diaries:
Book 1 - Claiming Victory
Book 2 - Sweet Victory
Book 3 - All For Victory

Book 4 - Chasing Victory
Book 5 - Lasting Victory
Book 6 - A Shackleford Victory
Book 7 - Final Victory will be released on 13th December 2024

The Admiral Shackleford Mysteries
Book 1 - A Murderous Valentine
Book 2 - A Murderous Marriage
Book 3 - A Murderous Season

Standalone Titles
An Officer and a Gentleman Wanted

ABOUT THE AUTHOR

Beverley Watts

Beverley spent 8 years teaching English as a Foreign Language to International Military Students in Britannia Royal Naval College, the Royal Navy's premier officer training establishment in the UK. She says that in the whole 8 years there was never a dull moment and many of her wonderful experiences at the College were not only memorable but were most definitely 'the stuff of fiction.' Her debut novel An Officer And A Gentleman Wanted is very loosely based on her adventures at the College.

Beverley particularly enjoys writing books that make people laugh and currently she has two series of Romantic Comedies, both contemporary and historical, as well as a humorous cosy mystery series under her belt.

She lives with her husband in an apartment overlooking the sea on the beautiful English Riviera. Between them they have 3 adult children and two gorgeous grandchildren plus a menagerie of animals including 4 dogs - 3 Romanian rescues of indeterminate breed called Florence, Trixie, and Lizzie, and a 'Chichon" named Dotty who was the inspiration for Dotty in The Dartmouth Diaries.

You can find out more about Beverley's books at www.beverley-watts.com

Printed in Great Britain
by Amazon